Wha
Abo

MW00883909

DEAD IN THE WATER

In *Dead in the Water*, R.J. Patterson accurately captures the action-packed saga of what could be a real-life college football scandal. The sordid details will leave readers flipping through the pages as fast as a hurry-up offense."

- **Mark Schlabach**
*ESPN college sports columnist and
co-author of* Called to Coach *and*
Heisman: The Man Behind the Trophy

"R.J. Patterson does a fantastic job at keeping you engaged and interested. I look forward to more from this talented author."

- *Aaron Patterson*
bestselling author of SWEET DREAMS

DEAD SHOT

"Small town life in southern Idaho might seem quaint and idyllic to some. But when local newspaper reporter Cal Murphy begins to uncover a series of strange deaths that are linked to a sticky spider web of deception, the lid on the peaceful town is blown wide open. Told with all the energy and bravado of an old pro, first-timer R.J. Patterson hits one out of the park his first time at bat with *Dead Shot*. It's that good."

- Vincent Zandri
bestselling author of THE REMAINS

"You can tell R.J. knows what it's like to live in the newspaper world, but with *Dead Shot*, he's proven that he also can write one heck of a murder mystery."

- Josh Katzowitz
NFL writer for CBSSports.com
& author of Sid Gillman: Father of the Passing Game

"Patterson has a mean streak about a mile wide and puts his two main characters through quite a horrible ride, which makes for good reading."

- Richard D., reader

DEAD LINE

"This book kept me on the edge of my seat the whole time. I didn't really want to put it down. R.J. Patterson has hooked me. I'll be back for more."

- *Bob Behler*

3-time Idaho broadcaster of the year and play-by-play voice for Boise State football

"Like a John Grisham novel, from the very start I was pulled right into the story and couldn't put the book down. It was as if I personally knew and cared about what happened to each of the main characters. Every chapter ended with so much excitement and suspense I had to continue to read until I learned how it ended, even though it kept me up until 3:00 A.M.

- *Ray F.*, reader

THE WARREN OMISSIONS

"What can be more fascinating than a super high concept novel that reopens the conspiracy behind the JFK assassination while the threat of a global world war rests in the balance? With his new novel, *The Warren Omissions*, former journalist turned bestselling author R.J. Patterson proves he just might be the next worthy successor to Vince Flynn."

- *Vincent Zandri*
bestselling author of THE REMAINS

Other titles by R.J. Patterson

Cal Murphy Thriller series

James Flynn Thriller series

Brady Hawk series

DEAD DROP

A Novel

R.J. PATTERSON

Dead Drop
© Copyright 2016 R.J. Patterson

This novel is a work of fiction. Names, characters, places, and incidents either are the product of the author's imagination or are used fictitiously. Any resemblance to actual persons, living or dead, events, or locales is entirely coincidental.

First Print Edition 2016
Second Print Edition 2017

Cover Design by Dan Pitts

Published in the United States of America
Green E-Books
PO Box 140654
Boise Idaho 83713

*For Klaus Berwald, the coach who instilled
in me a passion for the beautiful game*

CHAPTER 1

SID WESTIN ALWAYS CAREFULLY weighed his options—until now. The moment he formulated his ambitious plan to become the world's greatest soccer player, he knew he would never accomplish it through a series of haphazard events strung together by sheer luck. Such levels of greatness required a calculated effort to stick with a master plan, no matter how painful or how dire his future seemed. A smidgeon of good luck wouldn't hurt either. But Sid had failed—due to no fault of his own. And he didn't just know that because he was lying on the cold marbled floor at Puget Sound Bank with a gunman lurking above him.

Just a few hours before running this mundane errand for his wife, Sid was playing soccer in the front yard with his eight-year-old son.

"Dad!" yelled Mason. He was wearing his favorite shirt with a stingray on it, one they'd picked up after a recent trip to the Oregon Aquarium. "Dad! Look! Do you think I've got it now?"

Sid watched his son, who was working on a spin move with the soccer ball, and smiled and clapped. "Yes, Son, that's it. You've got it. If you perfect that move, you're going to be unstoppable."

Sid knew what it was like to be unstoppable. As a nine-teen-year-old, he made the roster for England's Under-20 team and scored five goals during the Under-20 World Cup held in Santiago. He was about to score his sixth and give England the lead in the Finals when an Argentine defender took him out on a reckless challenge. Three surgeries and eighteen months later, Sid still hadn't regained his promising form.

For more than a decade, he bounced around between lower-tier leagues in England, Germany, France, and Switzerland. Even though the doctors said he was fine, he knew he wasn't. He'd lost a step or two, vital in a game where a split second could make all the difference between scoring a goal and watching a shot get blocked by an oncoming defender. And for someone who was once labeled as "Norwich's Next Superstar," he was a disappointment to the fans of East Anglia.

However, when he moved to Seattle three years ago with his wife Rebecca, he discovered a newfound passion for soccer, rejuvenating his career—a career he thought might be over. With the United States' professional soccer league still in its relative infancy compared to the rest of the world, he took the opportunity offered to him to come play out his final days of competitive sport while serving as a mentor to the younger stars on the team. In the process, Sid exceeded expectations. Instead of being little more than a mentor to the young players, he became a star in his own right. He scored on a header in the final minute to knock Portland out of the playoffs in his first season and became an instant legend in Seattle.

That's not to say he didn't experience his share of trials in the Emerald City. His knee gave him problems after a hard tackle in the first game of his second season there. It required a minor surgery, but the setback seemed almost overwhelming to Sid. He considered retiring, but he soldiered on through rehabilitation and emerged stronger than ever. His age coupled with the speed of recovery also raised suspicion about the potential usage of performance enhancing drugs (PED), an accusation he vehemently denied. But all in all, he couldn't really complain about anything—almost anything.

A blaring horn a few feet away made him jump. Sid and Mason looked in the direction of the car to see Sid's wife, Rebecca, angrily waving a magazine at him as she roared up the driveway.

"Son, you stay here and keep practicing," Sid said. "I'm going to go check on your mum."

Sid hustled after her Cadillac Escalade, just fast enough to duck beneath the garage door that was closing. Alicia climbed out of the vehicle and immediately flung a Seattle weekly tabloid at him. She slammed the door and stormed inside.

He picked up the tabloid and read the headline—"He Shoots, He Scores?"—above a picture of Sid cozied up next to local television anchor, Sadie Livingston. Sid followed Rebecca inside.

"Is this what you're upset about?"

She didn't turn around, instead responding with a mocking tone, "Sid and Sadie."

"Come on. It's not like that, and you know it. That picture was from a fundraiser where someone asked me to pose with her."

"There were more pictures inside, pictures where you walked her outside."

"It was raining. I had an umbrella and she didn't. You know I'm a gentleman." He sighed. "I hardly even know her."

She rolled her eyes and shook her head, still refusing to turn around and look at him.

He grabbed her arms and gently turned her around so she could see him. "I swear. It was just an innocent photo."

Her eyes narrowed. "Innocent or not, I look like a fool."

He shoved aside the tabloid now lying on the kitchen counter. "Nobody believes anything in there. It's all rubbish. If I had known it would be on the front page, I never would've stopped to pose. Besides, it doesn't really matter—"

"It still matters to me."

He took a deep breath. "What I was saying is that it doesn't really matter what other people think. What's most important is what we think of each other, something that's far more powerful than a headline and a photo. We know each other—and I think if we're honest, we both know it's just a ridiculous insinuation."

She let out a long breath and continued putting away the groceries strewn across the kitchen counter. "Did you deposit that money into my account like I asked you to do? I need to pay for Mason's school tomorrow."

"I thought I showed you how to work the banking app so you could do it from here."

"The app isn't working—something about the operating system being updated, but their app hasn't updated yet and it's not compatible."

"Okay, fine. I'll go down there now."

Sid grabbed his keys and headed out the door. He jumped into his Porsche Carrera and put the top down. As he backed slowly out of the driveway, he motioned for

Mason to come near him.

"Where are you going, Dad?" Mason asked.

"Your mum asked me to run an errand for her."

"Can I come with you?"

"Not this time. But you keep working on that move of yours and show it to me when I get back. Deal?"

"Deal," Mason said as he flashed a grin. They bumped fists and Mason raced off, throwing the ball down and twirling around with it in an effort to impress his dad.

"Nice move, Son. Keep it up!" Sid said as he drifted slowly down the driveway. He jammed the gear into first and prepared to roar away. However, he didn't make it fifty feet until he noticed his neighbor staring at the back corner of her car just short of her driveway. He immediately stopped.

"Is everything all right, Mrs. Graham?"

She sighed and shook her head. "This just isn't my day," she said as she put her hands on her hips. "I swear if I was about to collect on a lottery ticket, I'd get hit by a train on the way there."

Sid turned his car off and hustled across the street to see how he could help her.

"What seems to be the problem?" he asked.

"I'm no mechanic, but it looks like a flat tire to me."

Sid craned his neck around the back corner of the car to concur with her assessment—and there was no denying it. The tire was completely deflated.

"Looks like you ran over something," he said as he knelt down next to the tire. He clawed at a cylindrical object sticking no more than a quarter of an inch beyond the tire's surface.

"What is it?" she asked as she leaned over his shoulder.

"I can't be sure yet, but it looks like a nail."

She muttered a few expletives under her breath. "All those damn construction zones on the highway."

"Well, don't get your knickers in a knot, Mrs. Graham," Sid said with a wink. "I've been known to change a tire or two in my day."

She clasped her hands together and smiled. "You'd do that for me?"

"Of course."

"But don't you have somewhere else to be?"

He waved dismissively at her. "I just have a short errand at the bank. Those thieves can wait."

She snickered and handed him the keys. "I'll go get you some lemonade."

"That's not really necessary, Mrs. Graham. I'm not that—"

The door slammed hard behind Mrs. Graham as she entered her house through the front door. Sid wasn't sure she really wanted to give him lemonade as much as she wanted to pick up her Pomeranian puppy, which hadn't stopped barking at the window since he crossed the street to help her.

Sid pulled out a set of tools from Mrs. Graham's trunk and then dropped to his knees to begin fixing the tire. His father had instilled in him the importance of helping others. It was a character flaw of his, according to Rebecca. She hated the fact that he always felt the need to play Good Samaritan, often causing them to be late for social functions as he couldn't resist helping someone who was broken down along the side of the road.

Fifteen minutes later, he finished changing the tire. Mrs. Graham thanked him before he drove off and headed toward the bank. He never even noticed the car that began following him.

***

SID'S PHONE RANG. It was Rebecca.

"Are you there yet?"

"Mrs. Graham had a flat tire, so I helped her with that before I left. I'm almost there."

"Your Good Samaritan act is getting old, Sid."

"Act? What are you talking about? I just wanted to help her. She's elderly, and her tire was flat. What else was I supposed to do—just drive by and leave her there?"

"Just hurry up, okay? We don't have all day."

Sid hung up and wondered how his marriage had reached this point. There was a time when Rebecca would've never spoken ill of him—to others or to his face. But those days had long since vanished, replaced by constant bickering and complaining about money. They had more than enough, but he could sense her disappointment with him every time the subject was broached. He'd never asked her point blank, but he figured she thought he was going to be a megastar and she'd be jetting between their beachfront house in Bali and their penthouse suite in London. Instead, they had just a modest 2,500 square foot house in the suburbs of Seattle and a small mountain cabin. He had shared her dreams, too, but he'd moved on years ago when he realized they would never be realized. He was satisfied with being a nominal star in the American pro soccer league—and she needed to be satisfied as well. But she wasn't. Not with the money. And not with him either. He'd held on as long as he could, mostly for Mason's sake. But Sid couldn't keep pretending. He had to admit the truth: his marriage was over.

He let out a long sigh and gazed out at the busy streetscape. The time had come. He made a quick phone call as he parked his car and closed the top. He climbed out and locked it with his key fob. He trudged along the sidewalk toward the bank's front doors. Despite his best efforts to remain anonymous in Seattle, it was impossible. Since the city had lost its NBA team in 2008, the football and soccer teams were the most popular professional franchises, respectively. Seattle's baseball team hadn't qualified for the playoffs in nearly two decades and was all but forgotten. And while soccer played second fiddle to football, it wasn't far behind.

Sid acknowledge a few awkward stares from people who looked as though they thought they knew him but weren't quite sure. Then a man wearing a Seattle FC jersey rushed over to him.

"Mr. Westin?" the man said.

Sid smiled. "Yes?"

The man clenched his first. "I knew it was you. I made a bet with a friend of mine over there that you were the Sid Westin."

"Congratulations on your victory, sir," Sid said.

The man nodded. "Oh, can you do me a favor?"

"A favor?"

"Yeah. Could you sign the back of my deposit slip?" the man said.

Sid laughed. "I'd be honored to." He scribbled on the piece of paper the man thrust into his hand. "Go Seattle FC."

"Thanks! And go Seattle FC!" the man replied as he hustled away.

The incident led to more awkward stares and whispers.

Sid didn't mind, welcoming a few other reluctant fans to sign whatever item they had on them.

One young boy wearing a Sounders' hat asked Sid to sign it for him.

He smiled at the kid. "How old are you?"

"Eight," he answered, flashing a toothless grin.

"Eight? That's how old my son is." Sid scribbled his signature on the boy's hat. "Are you playing soccer?"

The boy nodded. "One day, I want to be a star like you."

Sid tousled the boy's hair and grinned. "Just keep working hard. You never know."

Eventually, Sid made his way to the front of the line and asked the teller if he could transfer money between his accounts. She nodded and slid the paperwork to him.

"Just fill that out over there, and when you're finished, come back to me directly," she said. "No need for you to get back in line, Mr. Westin."

He strode toward a tall table and began entering the appropriate account numbers for the transaction. Before he could enter the last two numbers, a loud gunshot startled him.

Sid spun toward the direction of the sound and saw four masked gunmen firing their weapons in the air.

"On the ground, now!" roared one of the men as he fired a few more shots in the air.

Everyone in the bank hit the deck as ordered. The leader of the group jumped on top of the nearest counter.

"Nobody has to get hurt. All we want is the money. But if any of you think about being heroes, it's going to cost you. You understand me?"

Nobody said a word or moved.

"I said, 'Do you understand me?'"

The bank patrons all nodded, even Sid.

However, as Sid lay face down on the bank floor, he began to think about what was happening. He was witnessing an armed robbery, an event he could alter. For the moment, he couldn't tell if it was going to escalate into a hostage situation—but he had no intention of sitting around long enough to find out. He was going to turn the tables on them.

As the leader barked out orders, Sid waited for the right moment. He watched as the frightened employees shoveled stacks of cash into a bag some of the other robbers held open while the leader paced back and forth, still atop the counter.

The leader's pacing was rhythmic, almost lulling one to sleep. But not Sid. He watched this go on for nearly a minute until he determined the right moment to strike. Conjuring up all the gumption he had, he leapt to his feet and charged the leader. Only his long strides click-clacking on the marble floor alerted the leader that something was wrong.

The man spun and saw Sid racing toward him.

The leader didn't hesitate, firing once at Sid. The soccer star's momentum carried him forward as he crumpled to the ground, stopping just short of the counter. The man stooped down and looked at Sid. Using his foot, the leader turned over Sid's body and shook his head. Sid was clutching his side and gasping for air.

"I said, 'no heroes,' you idiot." The leader fired another shot, hitting Sid in the head.

He turned and whistled at his crew. "Let's go."

On the way out, the leader turned toward the security guard crouched in the corner and fired a shot, hitting him in the head.

"Thank you for your time, ladies and gentlemen," the leader said as they all stormed out the front door and into a waiting van.

Sid breathed shallowly as he felt the life slipping out of him.

"Just hang in there, Mr. Westin," one of the tellers said. "We're going to get you help."

Sid didn't move.

CHAPTER 2

CAL MURPHY CHECKED his rearview mirror and quickly changed lanes, squeezing between two cars as he kept pace with the late morning Seattle freeway traffic. He glanced at the clock and then at his wife, Kelly.

She put her hand on his knee. "Honey, we're going to make it to the airport in plenty of time."

Drawing a deep breath, he nodded. He caught a glimpse of Maddie in the backseat. She was clutching her MooMoo, the stuffed cow she wouldn't go anywhere without. He couldn't help but smile.

"Don't let her forget MooMoo at your mom's," Cal said to Kelly.

Her look turned serious. "That's why I bought an extra one the last time she lost it, remember? We're never going to endure that kind of torture again."

"You're always so prepared—that's why I'm so glad I married you."

"Is that the only reason you're glad you married me?"

Cal shook his head. "I don't have time to list all the reasons before we reach the airport."

She chuckled. "Nice save." After glancing out the window for a moment, she turned and looked at him. "How are you going to make it the next two weeks without me?"

"I don't know, but I'll manage somehow."

He turned on the radio just in time to catch the beginning of the sports news break on KJR 950 AM.

Enrique Gonzalez is due to be in court this afternoon for his arraignment. Gonzalez, the Mariners' leading hitter last season, was arrested for his role in an illegal gambling ring yesterday. If convicted, he faces up to fifteen years in federal prison…

His face fell as he listened to the news.

Kelly turned the radio off. "Cal, don't be so hard on yourself. You weren't the only person to believe his claims of innocence."

Cal pursed his lips and said nothing. His coverage of the Enrique Gonzalez gambling story wasn't the brightest moment in his journalism career. After a tip from someone he knew inside the FBI office telling him that Gonzalez was an unfortunate bystander in all of this but wouldn't be arrested, Cal interviewed Gonzalez about the allegations. His story painted a picture of Gonzalez being guilty only of picking friends of questionable character. And based on all the other facts and evidence Cal had pieced together regarding the case, it appeared that way to him as well. So, he wrote a story that all but said federal investigators had cleared Gonzalez of any wrongdoing and he was no longer part of the focus of their investigation.

Then Sabremetrics genius Mike Felton got involved. Felton, whose analysis of baseball statistics had helped him emerge from a hobby in his basement to a regular guest on ESPN, found some strange anomalies in Gonzalez's statistics. He compiled a list of games where Gonzalez's play appeared suspect and turned it over to the FBI. After leaning on a few suspects the FBI had taken into custody, the truth came out. Gonzalez was indeed working with the gamblers by tanking in several games. Cal was baffled by the allegations, especially since the star outfielder was making $18 million a year. It was a high risk with apparently not much reward. Gonzalez released a statement through his lawyer that he was innocent and the truth would come out. But Cal knew that if the FBI was going to charge him, the feds had a rock solid case that would withstand the challenge of top criminal defense attorneys and the skepticism of a jury. Then another one of his FBI sources told him they had a paper trail on Gonzalez that showed that his involvement in the gambling ring was minor compared to his ties to other organized crime bosses. Cal's source described Gonzalez as "an enterprising criminal who had parlayed his fame and wealth into something far more sinister." And Cal had bought Gonzalez's 100-watt smile and family man image, looking past the evidence that he normally would have scrutinized.

Cal shook his head. "In my gut, I knew something wasn't right. But I didn't trust it—and I only have myself to blame."

Once the news broke of Gonzalez's arrest—just two days after Cal's glowing article about him—*The Times* sports editor, Frank Buckman, yelled at Cal for fifteen minutes in Buckman's office, ranting about his irresponsible handling of the story. Cal took issue with his editor's accusations while agreeing with the conclusion: bad reporting jeopardizes the trust the newspaper has with its readers. While Cal concluded there wasn't much more he could've done to verify all of Gonzalez's story, short of talking with federal agents who couldn't comment during an ongoing investigation, at least he didn't have to write a story stating Gonzalez was exonerated of any wrongdoing.

"Well, don't beat yourself up over it, Cal," Kelly said as she patted him on the shoulder. "Just knock it out of the park on your next story—pun intended."

Cal forced a smile and glanced at her. "No, that right there is why I'm glad I married you."

He had a tendency to be hard on himself whenever he made a mistake, but she was right. The only thing he could do now was vow not to let it happen again and make his editor—and the newspaper's readers—forget all about his missteps with some award-winning caliber reporting on his next story.

He pulled up to the curb and put the car in park, hustling to the back and unloading Kelly and Maddie's luggage.

Kneeling down in front of Maddie, Cal looked her in the eyes. "You have fun with grandma, okay?"

"I will, Daddy," she said. "I'm gonna miss you."

"I'm gonna miss you too, pumpkin. Take care of Mommy for me."

She set down MooMoo so she could hug him tight with both hands. Cal tousled her hair and then watched her reach down and collect her stuffed cow.

He turned toward Kelly. "And don't you lose, MooMoo."

Kelly hugged him goodbye. "Don't get in any trouble while we're gone. Understand?"

"You know me."

"That's exactly why I said that," she said as she grabbed the handle on her suitcase and offered her hand to Maddie. "You know where to find me if you need help."

He waved again as Maddie looked over her shoulder for one final glimpse at him before disappearing through the sliding glass doors.

Cal slipped back into his car and pulled into one of the outer lanes. He hadn't driven two minutes before his phone rang. He answered it without looking at the screen.

"Did you forget something?" he asked.

"Forget something?" came the familiar voice. "Who do you think this is?"

Embarrassed that he didn't realize it was his editor on the other end of the call, Cal forced a laugh. "Sorry, Buckman, I just dropped my wife off at the airport. I thought she was calling me and telling me she'd forgotten something."

"If she did, she'll need to figure out a way to get it herself."

"Why? What's going on?"

"I need you on a story ASAP."

"What happened?"

"It's Sid Westin. He was killed earlier today."

"I'm on my way."

CHAPTER 3

DETECTIVE MEL KITTRELL APPROACHED the crime scene and slipped underneath the yellow tape cordoning off a small perimeter in front of Puget Sound Bank. He stopped and held it up for his partner, Eddie Quinn, who ducked beneath the tape and joined him on the other side. Several uniformed officers scurried out of the bank.

Phil Arledge, the sergeant who first responded to the scene, stood at the top of the bank steps and surveyed the area. He glanced down at Kittrell and Quinn as they made their way up the steps. "You ready for this?" he asked.

Kittrell shrugged and eyed the sergeant cautiously. "Would it make any difference if we weren't?"

"I've got half a mind to let one of those rookies take this case just because of your attitude," Arledge shot back.

"You sure it's got nothing to do with our last case?" Quinn said.

"Just don't screw this one up, okay? Both our jobs might be on the line if you do. Got it?" Arledge said.

Kittrell nodded and turned around to look at the officers interviewing witnesses and taking statements. A few feet away from the bottom of the steps, two officers were talking with the branch manager under the watchful eye of a man

Kittrell assumed was the bank president based on his expensive shoes and designer wool suit.

After taking in the scene, he followed Quinn into the building. Inside, the bank hummed with a bevy of activity. Picture taking. Bullet casing demarcations. Covering the deceased. The usual.

Lenny Young, one of the uniformed officers working the scene, hustled over to Kittrell and Quinn. "Hey, guys. Welcome to the party. This one is pretty nasty."

"I thought it was a basic armed robbery," Kittrell said.

"Sure. The crime itself was basic, but not one of the victims," Young said, gesturing for them to follow him. He pointed at the body. "See for yourself."

Kittrell knelt down and discreetly lifted the sheet draped over a lifeless body.

"You recognize him?" Young asked.

"Isn't this the famous soccer player from England?" Kittrell said, snapping his fingers. "Shawn? Or Simon?"

"Sid," Quinn said. "Sid Westin."

"Yeah. This is the guy?"

"The one and only," Young said.

Kittrell stood up. "Bastards shot him at point blank range."

"It appears that way," Young said.

"Anything else we need to know?"

Young nodded. "Follow me."

Kittrell and Quinn trailed Young as he led them across the bank toward another covered body. Kittrell crouched down and lifted the sheet.

"Security guard?"

Young nodded. "Sounds like they shot him on the way out just for fun. Witnesses said he never went for his gun."

"Your weapon never does you any good in your holster," Quinn said.

Kittrell put his hands on his hips and exhaled. "So, how did this go down?"

Young pointed back in the direction of Westin's body. "Four perps. The leader commanded the scene from atop the counter. It sounded pretty straightforward and was going down without a hitch until Sid Westin tried to play hero."

Kittrell's eyebrows shot upward. "Hero?"

"Yeah. Witnesses said he rushed the leader, who shot him point-blank right before he reached him. Dropped Westin right there."

"Why would he do that?" Quinn asked.

"Maybe he saw his opportunity to increase his brand if he brazenly stopped these guys," Young said.

Kittrell let out a long breath. "He's lucky he didn't get anyone else killed. You never know how these armed scum will react in a situation like that."

"Witnesses said the leader was very calm and in control. He warned everyone not to try anything."

"They always say that," Kittrell said. "That's Standard Bank Robbery 101."

"Well, at least it's not like your last case," Young said.

Kittrell shot Young a dirty look. "If you want all your teeth, I suggest you keep those kind of comments to yourself."

Young didn't flinch but stared back at Kittrell. "I'll be over there if you need me for anything."

Kittrell watched him walk away, glaring at him the whole way.

"Can you believe that guy?" Quinn said. "Like he's a perfect beat cop. I'd like to—"

"We can't screw this one up," Kittrell said. "Now, let's focus and see if we can find any more clues about who these guys are. Something tells me it won't be easy."

Kittrell walked the outer perimeter of the main bank lobby and searched for anything the crime scene crew might have missed since they began tagging and bagging all the evidence. As he strode around the room, he tried to focus and not get distracted by Arledge's and Young's comments. He tried not to take it personally, though it was nearly impossible. Over the past few weeks he'd received plenty of flack for his inability to capture Arnold Grayson, a serial killer who'd murdered six high-profile businessmen in the Seattle area over the past three years. He and Quinn arrested two men on suspicion of the murders, including one who was a high-level executive at one of the city's largest tech companies. Their blunders didn't play well publicly as the local media branded them the Emerald City's "Keystone Cops." *The Times* ran a big picture with the same moniker in large font above them. Nobody at the department was happy that they'd drawn such negative attention, especially the chief.

Kittrell and Quinn looked even worse when Grayson committed suicide by jumping off the Space Needle. He wrote a letter apologizing to the victims' families and listed each one, which turned out to be seven. When the media got wind that the serial killer had murdered more victims than the police first believed, it made the situation worse. Were they lying or just inept? That was the question hundreds of armchair detectives spent hours discussing on local radio talk shows.

Kittrell didn't help matters when a pushy reporter shoved a microphone in his face as he left the downtown precinct one day.

"At least we didn't shoot anybody," Kittrell said. And with that comment, he sparked another media firestorm that would undoubtedly fuel the news cycle for several more days.

Yet he was determined to make the department proud this time. He wasn't much of a soccer fan, but based on the way the city had embraced its soccer team, he knew this case was going to be a high-profile one. Everyone would want justice for Sid Westin—and he and Quinn were going to give it to them.

Kittrell stopped and looked down at something that appeared partially lodged beneath the molding at the foot of the teller counter. Stooping down, he slid the object out into the open with his pen, careful not to touch it. He slipped on a pair of latex gloves and examined what appeared to be a sports card. It contained Sid Westin's picture on one side and his statistics on the other.

Perhaps it was nothing. Or maybe it was the key to the case. At this point, it was simply a piece of evidence. But if he were going to get outsmarted again, it wouldn't be for negligence or lack of due diligence on his part.

No, these criminals wouldn't see him coming—and he wouldn't have his gun holstered either.

CHAPTER 4

REBECCA WESTIN POURED herself a glass of chardonnay and shifted back and forth on the stool. She slid the bottle down the bar to her friend Elizabeth, who'd stopped by to check on her. For Rebecca, Elizabeth's timing couldn't have been any better.

She kept one eye on Mason in the front yard, still working on his soccer skills.

"Oh, bloody hell, when is that pathetic excuse for a husband of mine going to be home?" Rebecca groused.

"Are you sure you want me to stay here until he arrives?" Elizabeth asked.

Rebecca nodded. "It'll keep me from murdering him."

She swept her hand across the counter, sending a small stack of papers flying.

"I know you're upset, Becs, but try to hold it together. If for anything, do it for Mason. Don't let him see you like this. Be strong."

"Is it wrong that I want him to know what a jerk his father is?"

Elizabeth patted her on the hand. "He's not a jerk of a father, just a husband, right?"

Rebecca rolled her eyes and sighed. "If you insist on

keeping me from being pissed off, I just might kick you out."

"I'm not saying you can't be upset, but just keep it under control. You don't want to do anything you'll regret."

"Already too late for that," Rebecca said as she took another gulp of her wine. "I married Sid." She teared up but waved her hands in front of her eyes.

"It's okay to cry."

"No. I'm not going to shed one tear for him. He's a bastard, serving me divorce papers right in front of Mason, papers that accused me of infidelity. He needs to get off his self-righteous high horse." Rebecca grabbed the tabloid at the end of the bar and held it up. "Here he is running around the city with all these beautiful women and just shrugs like it's no big deal—and he acts like nothing is going on." She slammed the paper on the bar. "He's full of it. I know for a fact he's had at least two affairs since we've been married."

"Two affairs? Are you sure? Why are you still with him?"

"I never caught him, but I suspected him at least twice. He was acting strange, and when I confronted him about it, he denied it all. But I'm no idiot."

"Did he ever cheat on you while you were dating?"

She shook her head. "He was the perfect gentleman. But that's how they reel you in. They act like you're a queen and then they dump you for the next hot woman that comes along. Men are scum, I tell you. All of 'em. And if I—"

Rebecca stopped mid-sentence when she saw Elizabeth making a strange face. She then heard the door slam shut and watched Mason shuffle toward her.

"Mum? Is everything okay?" he asked.

"Yes, yes. Everything is fine. Why do you ask?"

"There's a policeman in our front yard."

Rebecca got up and peered out the window. "That's

strange. Why don't you go clean up for supper?"

Mason bent over and picked up a handful of the papers strewn about the floor. "What's this?"

She snatched it out of his hands. "Oh, it's nothing, Son. Go get cleaned up like I said."

He scampered upstairs and was out of earshot when an officer rapped on the front door.

"What do you think that's all about?" Elizabeth asked.

Rebecca shrugged and walked toward the door to open it. "My day can't get any worse, no matter what it is."

"Can I help you?" she asked.

A pair of officers stood at her door. The officer closest to the door looked down, holding his hat in his hand. "May I come in, Mrs. Westin?"

"What's this all about? You're starting to scare me."

"It's about your husband."

She gestured for both officers to come inside. "What about him?"

The officer stepped inside and swallowed hard. "You might want to sit down for this."

"No, tell me what you came here to say about my husband right now. Is he in jail or the hospital?"

"No, ma'am. Your husband was shot today during a bank robbery, and he passed away before any medical help arrived. I'm really sorry, Mrs. Westin."

Rebecca staggered toward the couch. She couldn't believe the swirling emotions inside her. A few minutes ago, she would've killed him herself if she had the chance. But now?

She started to sob. Elizabeth sat down next to Rebecca, placing her arm around her grieving friend.

"Thank you, officer," Elizabeth said.

He handed her his card. "I'm sure you'll have more questions later. Tell her she's free to call me whenever she feels up to it to discuss all the details and what funeral home she wants us to deliver his body to." He paused. "I'll show myself out. Again, I'm really sorry, Mrs. Westin."

Rebecca didn't look up at him, continuing to sob.

"What is it, Mum?" Mason said as he descended the stairs.

She didn't answer.

"Mum, what's wrong?"

***

THREE HOURS LATER, Rebecca was starting her second bottle of wine and had no intention of stopping. She slumped into a chair in the living room and wiped away another set of streaking teardrops.

Elizabeth came down the stairs and settled onto the couch.

"Is he asleep?" Rebecca asked.

"It took him a while, but he finally stopped crying and fell asleep."

"Thank you for staying with me."

"Do you want me to stay here tonight? I can call Bill and ask him to drop over some clothes."

Rebecca shook her head. "No, you go home and kiss your husband. You don't need to wallow with me in my misery all night."

"Just promise me you'll stop drinking, Becs, okay? That's not going to help you tonight."

"It'll help me sleep."

Elizabeth picked up her coat and sighed. "I'm not your

mother, but please consider what I've asked, all right?"

"Fine," Rebecca said as she put her glass down on the coffee table in front of her. "I'll take your advice."

"I'll call you in the morning. I'll clear my schedule and help you do whatever you need help with."

Rebecca got up and hugged her friend again. "You're the best."

Her phone started buzzing on the coffee table.

"Don't answer that unless you want to," Elizabeth said. "And don't be afraid to tell people that you just need some time."

"I won't. Don't worry."

Elizabeth gave her another quick hug before exiting.

Rebecca locked the door behind her and walked back into the living room where her phone was still buzzing.

She glanced at the name on the caller ID. It was normally something that would make her smile, but not tonight.

"My god, Becs, are you okay? I heard it on the news."

"I'll be fine, just more relieved than anything that it's over. The bastard served me divorce papers this afternoon after he disappeared and went to the bank."

"Well, you won't have to worry about him any more."

Rebecca picked up her glass of wine and took another sip. "Is it a good idea for you to be calling me right now?"

"Nobody is going to catch us. I've been good about covering my tracks. Besides, there's nothing odd about me calling you tonight. It'd be expected, in fact."

"I hope you're right. I've got enough things to worry about right now."

"Well, at least you won't have to go through a nasty public divorce now, will you?"

She forced a smile. She wanted it to be more authentic

than it was, though she still wasn't sure she should be exhibiting any signs of happiness at the moment. If anyone were watching her, she wouldn't want them to get the wrong idea—or the right one.

CHAPTER 5

CAL SCROLLED THROUGH his Twitter feed and resisted the urge to write back to at least a half dozen classless responses to his post about Sid Westin's death. Cal felt his blood pressure rising as he kept reading. He was breaking one of his hard and fast rules: never read the comments. But he also had another rule that required him to: always keep a pulse on your readers.

In half an hour, the Seattle Football Club—or Seattle FC as they were more commonly known—would commence a press conference detailing anything they'd learned from police about Westin's death and how they planned to honor him. If it had been any other player, Cal suspected they would've waited for another day or two before commenting publicly. But Sid Westin wasn't just any other player.

Cal interviewed Westin for a feature story less than two years ago and spent an entire day with him. He got to know Westin's son and nanny when he hung out at his house. He met everyone in the family except Rebecca, who was out of town playing at a charity golf tournament. The profile article was well received and helped Cal curry favor with Westin. Not that Cal was trying to do that, but he generally liked Westin after following him around and meeting his family—

and that came across in the piece Cal wrote. Cal smiled as he remembered how Westin had locked his keys in his car that day and caused him to be late for practice by fifteen minutes. Westin just shrugged it off. "See, Cal, I'm a normal guy," he said while they waited on his nanny to bring him his extra set of keys.

But based on law enforcement's initial reading of the situation around Westin's heroic attempt, he wasn't so normal. Cal knew the normal guys who were in the bank were still alive today.

Cal continued to swipe up on his phone and review the comments until he saw one that gave him reason to pause and re-read it: "He had it coming to him."

Who would say such a thing about a guy who was beloved by all? Cal realized apparently not everyone was fond of Westin as he—and most of Seattle—was. If Cal was going to write an authentic memorial piece on Westin, he had to mention his detractors. And Westin had his fair share of people who disliked him. Some fans didn't like the fact that Seattle FC was getting English leftovers, and a player who'd been plagued with injuries on top of that. There were also others who hadn't forgiven him for missing a penalty kick against the L.A. Galaxy that would've sent Seattle FC through to the MLS Cup final two years ago. But this nasty response to Westin seemed rude and insensitive and likely nothing more.

But that jogged Cal's memory about his most recent conversation with Westin. He'd been at the Seattle FC training facility a few days earlier and saw Westin walking toward his car.

"Did you remember your keys this time?" Cal asked.

Westin chuckled and unlocked the car. "I keep an extra

set in my locker just in case I don't. There might be some time when my nanny isn't available to help me."

"Always be prepared, right?" Cal said with a smile.

"Except when a reporter is following you around for a day to document your life."

"So, how are you?"

"I'm doing okay, but things have been strange lately."

Cal cocked his head. "Strange? How?"

"I don't know. I can't shake this feeling that I'm being watched, like somebody is after me."

"Is there a reason someone would be after you?"

"None that I know of. I try not to make enemies, though sometimes you just can't help it."

"You received any threats or strange communications?"

Westin shook his head. "I can't recall any, though I've had about a half-dozen calls in the past week where no one answers once I pick up. It's kind of unsettling."

"A stalker perhaps?"

"I guess anything is possible. It's just got me a little edgy."

Cal didn't think much of the conversation at the time, but now it seemed pertinent given the circumstances. Maybe the shooting was premeditated.

Five minutes later, he was in his boss's office, sharing his hunch with him.

"Cal, I know you don't want to get burned again because of what happened on that Enrique Gonzalez story—I get that. But concocting something that isn't there isn't how to go about atoning for that. Just go write a good story and properly honor Westin."

"I have no plans to concoct anything. I just want to ask a few questions, see if anything seems off."

Buckman drummed his fingers on his desk and looked down pensively before looking up at Cal. "Look, you know what happens in cases like these. You start inquiring about something that makes his teammates or other people in the front office nervous or worse—they start seeing something that was never really there. Or you just might happen to talk to the one guy on the team that wouldn't mind seeing Westin's reputation tarnished. Then what? It's just not the way you should approach this story; I don't care how many awards you've won."

Cal nodded but he wasn't in agreement.

***

CAL WATCHED INTENTLY AS Fred Jameson placed both hands on the podium and looked down at his notes for a few moments. The Seattle FC president and CEO slid some papers around and then took a deep breath before finally looking up at the media members packed tightly in the press conference room. Usually, he spoke to no more than a handful of writers and television and radio reporters. But today, every media outlet seemed to send multiple people.

"We all know why we're here today," Jameson began. "Our entire organization wishes it was under different circumstances. Losing one of our own isn't just an event in the news cycle. For us, it's deeply personal. On some level or another, we all spent time with Sid Westin. Like any workplace, there were those of us who knew him better than others. But we're all really hurting right now. While I intend to share more stories at the funeral about the great man Sid was, I can tell you now that he touched all of our lives in various ways. He was a star not just on the field but off the field as well, especially in the way he treated others."

Jameson expounded on Sid's greatness for a few more minutes before yielding the podium to Paul Holloway, the media relations director for Seattle FC.

"Thank you for your patience during this time," Holloway said. "It's been difficult for us all. Now, I know that many of you have questions, some of which we can't answer and others of which should be answered by our local law enforcement. But at this time, we want you to respect the people within this organization and the players. We're all grieving. Therefore, we won't be making any players available over the next week. We also want to announce that we've canceled Saturday's game against Dallas and will reschedule it for later in the season."

Jameson continued, but Cal wasn't interested in sticking around to hear any more of it. He slipped out the back and eyed a couple of players kicking the ball around on a practice field.

One of the players, Javier Martinez, jogged over in Cal's direction. Martinez wasn't the biggest star on the team, but he was a crowd favorite. Born in Seattle to immigrant parents, Martinez had remained in Seattle for almost every season of his playing career. With the exception of a one-year stop at a California junior college to get his grades up, Martinez starred at the University of Washington and led the school to a pair of conference championships. Seattle FC signed him as a free agent once he graduated, and he was easily the best feel-good story on the team. The only complaint anyone ever had against him was his spotty play since turning pro. Some games he played like an all-star; other games he played like his mind was in another place. And while it maddened fans, most who knew Martinez's story were forgiving. His father, who worked in the shipping yard at the docks, had been arrested one too many times and was deported six months after Javier signed with Seattle FC. It seemed to weigh heavily on the younger Martinez. And while soccer wasn't Cal's beat, it was one of the most well-known stories among the city's sports fans due to *The Times'* coverage.

Apparently, he didn't get the memo that he's not supposed to speak to me.

Cal flashed a brief smile and offered his hand to Martinez. "Good to see you, Javy, though I wish it was under different circumstances."

"I know what you mean. Everyone is torn up about it. We were great friends, you know."

"Well, I'm sorry for your loss. I liked Sid too and had a decent rapport with him." Cal glanced at his notes. "So, what are you gonna miss the most about him?"

Martinez's head dropped as he glanced down at the field and thought for a moment. "I'm gonna miss his kindness and compassion. He was our team leader in every way. I loved the guy."

"Did he ever talk to you about having any enemies?"

"He often complained that his biggest enemy was time and how she'd been so cruel to him, allowing him to build his dreams only to have them torn down over time."

"But no personal enemies?"

Martinez cocked his head to one side and furrowed his brow. "You mean like people who didn't like him?"

Cal nodded.

"Is there something you know that you're not telling me? It was a straight bank robbery with an unfortunate ending, right?"

"Is that the story all my media brethren are pumping out?"

"It's the story you wrote, too."

"Perhaps I was wrong. Consider for a moment that it wasn't so random. Who were some of the teammates who had it out for Sid?"

Martinez rubbed his eyes and sighed. "To be perfectly honest, I wasn't surprised to hear that he was dead. I half expected it—just not like that."

"So, is there one person in particular that has perhaps harbored enough ill will toward Sid to conceive and execute such a plan?"

Martinez shrugged. "Go talk to Matt Norfolk. His locker was right next to Sid's. Plus, they had some issues."

Cal nodded and walked across the field toward Norfolk, who was kicking the ball toward an open net from about fifty feet away. As he headed toward his next interview subject, Cal recalled the rumors he'd heard about the Westin-Norfolk feud that had escalated over the last year. When the story was first related to him, Cal assumed the conflict was about jealousy. Sid took over Norfolk's slot in the starting lineup and never relinquished it. Instead of taking the issue up with his coach, Norfolk decided to take it up directly with Sid. According to witnesses of Norfolk's confrontation with Sid, the situation tense. But Cal never knew if there was something deeper to their rift than playing time.

Just as Cal was about to ask Norfolk directly, Holloway exited the press conference and shouted excitedly at Cal as he crossed the field.

"I thought I said no interviews," Holloway said. "How much clearer do I need to make it for you, Cal?"

Cal sighed and shook his head before pulling out his

notebook and scribbling down a few thoughts onto paper.

Did Matt Norfolk hate Sid Westin enough to fake a robbery and use that as an excuse to murder him?

It was a question that popped into Cal's head. Suddenly, he wanted it answered—and soon.

CHAPTER 6

KITTRELL KICKED HIS FEET UP on his boss's desk and leaned back as he awaited the arrival of Ted Roman, the department's Chief of Police. While Kittrell enjoyed a strong rapport with Roman before he botched the serial killer case, their relationship had since weakened. But that didn't stop Kittrell from needling Roman, who had a reputation around the department for being a neat freak.

Quinn sat in a chair in the corner of the room, leaning forward as he eyed Kittrell. "You sure you wanna do that?" Quinn said, gesturing toward Kittrell's feet. "We need to get back on his good side, remember?"

Kittrell didn't move. "Roman loves us—and this is how I endear myself to him?"

"By annoying him?"

"It's what partners do to each other."

"What are you trying to say?"

Kittrell sighed. "I'm not trying to say anything. I'm telling you that this is how partners act." He paused for a moment. "You annoy me all the time."

"How?"

"You like Justin Bieber."

Quinn cocked his head and furrowed his brow. "Really?

How do you find that annoying? Everyone loves Justin Bieber."

"No, they don't. And I dare say that you'd be lucky to find more than two men in the department who find his music appealing. It sounds like a whiny, jilted teenaged girl singing, but just an octave lower."

"I understand not everyone is a Belieber, but—"

"Okay," Kittrell said, interrupting him. "That right there. I'm going to ask for a transfer now."

"What?" Quinn said, throwing his hands in the air. "What did I say?"

"You used the word *Belieber*. You might as well have drug your fingernails down the chalkboard and chanted the word *moist* while you danced to a Justin Bieber song."

Quinn sat back in his seat. "I get the sense you don't like Bieber."

"Well, you are my crack detective partner."

Quinn broke into a smile. "No matter how hard of a time you give me here, your rationale for propping your feet on top of Roman's desk is ridiculous."

"How's that?"

"You two aren't partners—and I guarantee you that he won't like it."

A faint grin spread across Kittrell's lips. "We'll see about that."

A few moments later, the door flew open and Roman shuffled inside. When he turned around, his eyes went straight for Kittrell's feet. "How many times do I have to tell you that I hate it when people mess up my desk?" He pulled Kittrell's feet off his desk and gestured for him to get up. Kittrell complied and sat down next to Quinn as they both watched Roman open up the bottom right drawer on his desk and pull out a bottle of some cleaning agent and a rag.

Roman squirted the liquid onto his desk and scrubbed the spot furiously. "So, what are you boys doing in my office so early? I hope you've found something on the robbery."

"As soon as we do, you'll be the first to know, sir," Kittrell said.

Roman didn't look up as he continued to clean. "Have you heard from forensics yet on the casings found at the scene?"

Quinn pulled his chair closer to Roman's desk. "Not yet."

"What about the autopsy? Have we heard anything back from the coroner on that?"

Kittrell sighed. "Still waiting for that, too."

Roman stopped cleaning and finally looked up at the two detectives across the desk from him. "So, what have you been doing? Creating some plausible scenarios about who the perps are and why they attacked this particular bank? Have you done anything that's going to help us catch them? I've got to speak to the press soon, and I need to give them an update—or at least give off the impression that you two are doing your jobs and aren't going to let the department and this city down again."

Kittrell leaned forward. "Sir, if I may, I—"

"You may find out what's going on, Kittrell. That's what you may do."

"Look, just indulge me for a moment, okay?"

Roman opened his drawer and dug out a toothpick before sliding it between his lips. "Go ahead."

"What if Sid Westin was actually the target instead of the bank? What if the bank was just a red herring to distract us from a brazen murder?"

Roman's eyes narrowed. "That's not asking me to indulge a theory; that's asking me to believe lunacy."

"But, sir, there's more, and if you—"

"That's enough." Roman turned his gaze toward Quinn. "You agree with this cockamamie theory?"

Quinn shrugged. "I agree that it's not likely, but it's still worth checking out. I don't think anyone in this department wants another person to get away with murder, do we?"

"Of course not. But this isn't a homicide case; this is a damn bank robbery gone bad. Your job is to figure out a way to find the punks who were behind this so we can arrest them for armed robbery and murder. You're both good detectives. Now go do your job."

Kittrell stood and put his head down as he exited the office, followed by an equally subdued Quinn.

"That went over well," Kittrell said.

"You would've been better off just keeping your feet on his desk," Quinn quipped.

They turned toward their desks when one of the uniformed officers approached Kittrell. "Detective, we just received a call on the tip line that you might be interested in hearing. I put the recording to your voicemail."

Kittrell hustled toward his desk and slid into his chair, while Quinn sat on top of Kittrell's desk. Kittrell dialed his voicemail and switched to the speakerphone as they listened in.

"I'm calling about Sid Westin's death at the robbery that took place earlier this week," said the voice of a nervous male caller. "I—I—I just wanted to say that there may be more to this. I know that Sid was about to be outed for using performance-enhancing drugs. And"—there was a pause with some rustling going on in the background—"there's more, but I can't say any more. Gotta go." Click.

Kittrell hung up and spun around in his chair to look at Quinn. "What do you make of that?"

"I'm not sure. What are you thinking?"

Kittrell shrugged. "There could be something to it. I think we both agree that it's possible that this was more than just your cut-and-dry armed robbery, though we're not sure what yet. Maybe this is the key."

"Or maybe it's someone trying to punk us after the Arnold Grayson case."

Kittrell held his index finger in the air. "That's a possibility we can't rule out either. Sorting through the crap in this case isn't going to be easy. But I think we ought to wait until the report comes out before we start building theories around an anonymous call from the tip line."

Quinn nodded and got up before returning to his desk.

Kittrell pulled out his notebook and jotted down a few notes. He publicly stated his position on the tip, holding it suspect. But, privately, the gears inside his head were whirring. This was the break he'd been hoping for.

Now, it was just a matter of constructing a believable theory and pitching it to Quinn and Roman as Kittrell began the investigation. And it wouldn't be easy.

CHAPTER 7

BILL LANCASTER RUBBED HIS HANDS together as he waited for the FBI agents to enter the room. The doctor glanced at his hands, which had started to bead with sweat. Patting his hands dry on his pants, he stared at the two-way mirror directly in front of him. He knew they were watching, but he couldn't make the color return to his face or appear less nervous. If they revealed their strategy, he might relax— but not a second sooner. He couldn't fake courage.

For the past few months, he'd been wondering when this encounter would take place. A friend at the St. Louis FBI field office warned him that they were looking into him and that he better make sure everything he was doing was above board. It was common courtesy, though also illegal. But Lancaster took the tip seriously, which enabled him to tweak his records. He couldn't make them look perfect for fear that they would investigate further. Instead, he decided to plant a red herring and send them off in pursuit of a lead that would take them nowhere. He would get a slap on the wrist, if anything at all. It was all very simple—a forged signature by a doctor for a prescription to a Major League Baseball player who'd already been convicted of using illegal prescriptions. Lancaster dug through his phone records to find the date the scrupulous doctor's office had called him and faxed him something. With the doctor already in jail, it wouldn't be enough to cause the feds to spend thousands of dollars in time and resources to pursue such a claim. Lancaster's invention had nothing to do with the athlete, of course, but it would lend veracity to his forthcoming statement, one he'd rehearsed a thousand times since the FBI served him with a search warrant and carted out boxes of records. He'd claim he was simply filling a prescription for the office when it was out of the drug. If that were the impending line of questioning, the interrogation would run smoothly and rather harmlessly. Yet the uncertainty of it all was why Lancaster hadn't relaxed for even a moment as he fidgeted in his seat.

When agent Al Hollister entered the room with his partner Bart Zellers, neither one of them appeared to have any intention of putting Lancaster at ease. There was no cordial greeting or small talk; it was all business.

Hollister dropped a manila folder on the table and then slid it toward Lancaster.

Lancaster put his hands on top of the folder—palms down—and dragged it in front of him. "Am I supposed to know what this is?"

"You tell me," Hollister shot back as he eyed Lancaster. "Go ahead. Open it."

Slowly, Lancaster reached for the curled corner of the folder and grabbed it with his thumb and forefinger. He pulled it open and tried to hide his shock. There was nothing about the disgraced and convicted doctor or the baseball player. Instead, staring back at him was a copy of an order his office fulfilled and shipped out. He never considered for even one moment that this order would attract the scrutinizing eye of the sharpest FBI agent. The HGH levels in the prescription order were within legal ranges. However, the frequency was a day or two earlier than was legal. He'd already planned to dismiss it as a clerical error or give the standard, "I'm sure there's a reasonable explanation for this. We would never knowingly break the law."

But that would be a lie. He would knowingly break the law, and he wouldn't give it a second thought. For Lancaster, he lived by the carpe diem mantra. Or in his case, seize the money. Though it was really about something else entirely. A soccer player needed help, and Lancaster was happy to oblige, even if it was illegal.

It'll be virtually undetectable to some FBI analyst combing through my records.

Lancaster was wrong, as evidenced by the piece of paper lying on the table right in front of him. They'd caught him, and he had no plausible explanation—at least not one on the tip of his tongue. He needed to stall.

Lancaster furrowed his brow and stared at the sheet of paper. "What exactly am I looking at here? I'm afraid that I'm not too familiar with shipping records and practices. That's not my department."

Deep breath, Bill. You can do this.

Hollister leaned forward on the table and clasped his hands. "Dr. Lancaster, please dispense with the naivety act. This is very much a part of your business, and I think you're very well aware of why this was flagged during our investigation."

"I'm sure if this is true, then perhaps there's some reasonable explanation for it all."

Hollister leaned back and crossed his arms. "Enlighten me."

"A glitch in the computer system perhaps. Our orders are automated."

"Need I remind you that this conversation is being

recorded right now?"

"Are you charging me with something? Because if you are, I'd like to see my lawyer."

Zellers, who'd been observing quietly in the corner of the room, stepped forward and broke his silence. "We're just asking you a few questions, Dr. Lancaster. If this is all just some big misunderstanding, we'd love for you to clear it up for us." He glanced at his watch. "I've got reservations at Machiano's tonight at seven. Make my wife happy, and explain it all to us."

"I am giving you the most reasonable explanation I can think of."

Hollister's eyes narrowed as he used his index finger to tap the papers he'd placed in front of Lancaster. He took over the questioning with an aggressive stance toward Lancaster. "Do you recognize the name on this document? A Mrs. Rebecca Westin? Of all the clients—"

"Patients, Agent Hollister. I have patients."

"Of all the clients, why was it her? Why didn't your system goof up someone who lived in, say, Timbuktu, Nebraska? Why was it specifically Rebecca Westin in Seattle? Explain that one to me."

"I really think I need my lawyer before we go any further."

"Oh, sure. Go hide behind your lawyer. That doesn't make you look guilty at all."

Lancaster felt the blood rush to his face. In a flash, he went from irritated to angry. "I don't know what kind of witch hunt you're on, Agent Hollister, but you're not going to get me to admit to anything I didn't do. Not now, not ever."

Zellers put his hand on Hollister's shoulder and spoke calmly, "If you cooperate, we can make sure the judge goes easy on you. You'll lose your license, but you won't spend the better part of your life in prison."

"I didn't commit any crime, at least not knowingly. And if the FBI wants to exhaust all of its resources just to prove I'm innocent, by all means, go ahead. I'll happily file a countersuit to recoup all my lawyer fees and embarrass both of you. If this was your big attempt to get me to admit to your asinine theory, you two are in far more trouble than you realize right now."

Zellers sighed. "We aren't trying to coerce a confession, Dr. Lancaster. That would be illegal. We are simply extending you an opportunity to admit to the truth before this investigation goes any further and we uncover more unpleasant things for you."

"More unpleasant than what? Than this? Having my integrity and practice questioned is as unpleasant as it could ever get for me."

Hollister stood up. "Oh, trust me. It can get far more unpleasant, especially when it comes out that several high profile Seattle athletes have recently tested positive for HGH. None of it has been made public yet. We've been working with various league officials to keep it under wraps so we could flush out the source." He gestured toward Lancaster. "And look what we found."

"How does it feel to grasp at straws?" Lancaster asked. "You two are pathetic, wasting my time and taxpayers' precious dollars. Charge me, or we're done here."

Zellers motioned toward the door.

Lancaster didn't linger for even a moment, storming out of the room and marching down the hall toward the exit. He didn't know if his act convinced them to dig deeper or to drop the case. Under his breath, he prayed it was the latter.

CHAPTER 8

CAL WOKE UP to a buzzing cell phone. He rolled over and picked up the phone, squinting as he looked at the image on the screen. Kelly's face was staring back at him.

"Do you have any idea what time it is?" he mumbled.

"Yeah, it's nine," she said before realizing her mistake. "Oh, Cal, I'm sorry. The time difference slipped my mind. I hadn't talked with you and just wanted to find out how things were going."

He moaned. "You know better than to call me this early. I'm a grouch until I've had my first cup of coffee."

"I know, I know. I'm sorry. I totally forgot." She paused. "But now since you're up, do you wanna talk?"

Cal scratched the sleep out of his eye with the index finger on his free hand. He tried to change his disposition, something he'd only do for Kelly. "Sure, I'd love to. Are you guys having a good time?"

"Believe it or not, it's been wonderful so far. Me and Mom haven't gotten into a single argument."

"Well, that's good news."

"Yeah. And Maddie is having a great time. She's getting to visit some of her favorite playgrounds here."

"Maddie remembers those playgrounds? She was barely

two years old when we left."

"I don't know. She says she remembers them."

Cal laughed. "Does she remember the day she was born?"

"Oh, Cal. Don't be hard on her. She's just trying to be big."

"I know, but I want to keep her as little as possible for as long as possible. Is there anything wrong with that?"

"I'm right there with you, hon. But just cut her some slack and play along when she talks to you, okay?"

"Fine. Your wish is my command."

"How's your coverage of the Sid Westin death? It was big news out here on the East Coast, too."

"I don't know. It's going okay, but I've got a funny feeling about this."

"What do you mean by that? It's just a few reaction stories, right?"

"It could be—or it could be something much more."

"Now, Cal, don't go poking your nose where it doesn't belong and wind up shot or kidnapped."

"I'm always cautious. You know me."

She sighed. "Yes, I do know you, and that's why I feel obligated to say such a thing."

"All right, all right. You win." He held up his hand as if he were swearing an oath, even though she couldn't see him. "I promise to be cautious."

"Good. Now that we've got that settled, why do you feel uneasy about the story?"

"It's not that I feel uneasy about it as much as I think there's more to it—like perhaps Westin was the intended target rather than the vault."

"Is Buckman on board with your theory?"

"Not exactly. He keeps telling me to drop it."

"But not Cal Murphy," she quipped.

"Exactly. Something is a little hinky about it all."

"Hinky? Since when did you start using the word hinky?"

"My word choice is bothering you now? First I'm giving Maddie a hard time; now my vocabulary isn't to your liking. Man, I can't win for losing today."

She chuckled. "Just think what it would be like if I was actually there."

He scanned the room, which more closely resembled a volcanic closet that had erupted and spewed clothes down the mountainside. It wouldn't send the natives running for cover, but it would send him running for his life if Kelly saw the sudden onset of a pigsty. "It'd be better than living the bachelor life—that's for sure." He couldn't see her, but he knew she was smiling.

"So, what seems so hinky about this story?"

"I don't know, but he certainly wasn't beloved by all his teammates."

"Horror of horrors," she said in a mocking tone. "Somebody didn't like Sid Westin."

"Stop it. You're the one who asked."

She turned more serious. "Well, it doesn't sound like much at the moment beyond what we know happened."

"When you put it that way, it does sound like I'm about to lose my mind. But the truth of the matter is he wasn't universally loved." He paused. "Just don't tell Maddie. She'll be crushed that not everyone worships Sid Westin like she does."

"I'd let you not tell her yourself, but she's out having too much fun on the playground."

"Don't interrupt her then, but I'd love to talk with her at some point later today. Just have fun and be good with your mom, okay?"

"Always."

Cal laughed to himself before bidding her goodbye and hanging up. "Always. I know better."

The conversation energized him enough to get up and begin his day. He still had a few rocks he wanted to turn over and inspect before resigning himself to the fact that the obvious answer was indeed the actual one.

***

AFTER CAL HAD SHOWERED and finished his first cup of coffee, his phone rang again. This time, it was a number he didn't recognize.

"This is Cal Murphy."

"Mr. Murphy?"

"Yes?"

"My name is Alicia Westin, Sid Westin's younger sister."

Cal knew exactly who she was. Someone in *The Times'* features department wrote a story about her and how she'd left everything in England to start over and follow her brother's soccer career in Seattle. She was devoted to her brother, if anything. "Oh, yes, Alicia, I know who you are. Hi. I'm truly sorry for your loss."

"Thank you, kind sir. I appreciate the gesture. But I'm afraid that there might be more to his death than we realize, and it's something I want to see resolved before I can truly lay him to rest, mentally speaking."

"I understand. Go on."

"After knowing what I know about Sid's history with

some of the other players on the team, it's completely plausible that this was a deliberate attempt on his life."

"I'm not saying I disagree with you, but what kind of information do you have that's making you suppose such a thing happened?"

"A few days ago, I remarked about how cute Matt Norfolk was. It's not the first time I tried to worm my way into getting a date with a professional soccer player."

"And what does this have to do with your suspicions of foul play?"

"Sid told me to stay the hell away from Matt Norfolk and threatened me if I dared to go against him."

"So, your brother thought Matt Norfolk was a sketchy individual?"

"Yes, and he told me other things about him too."

"Such as?"

"Such as Matt confronted Sid once after practice and told him he was going to take his job and then his livelihood for how he was treated. Sid obviously never lost his job. But guess who's starting now?"

"Perhaps it's Matt Norfolk."

"I'd like to string that little punk up for what he did to my brother."

"Now, Alicia, if there's one thing I've learned in investigating a story like this, it's important not to rush to judgment—from any side. Don't even form a serious hypothesis until you've heard all the facts."

"I've heard enough—like Matt told Sid to go back to England."

"While that's interesting, it's hardly proof that he attempted something so malevolent as murder."

"Don't ever underestimate a spurned soccer player."

Cal chuckled to himself. "I'll keep that in mind. Thanks for the call."

Once he hung up, Cal smiled. He wasn't taking his own advice. He'd created a theory before he heard both sides of the story, and her claim was starting to fit neatly into it. It wasn't solid journalism—yet. But it was an interesting theory to explore.

And that's exactly what he intended to do.

CHAPTER 9

MEL KITTRELL FELT THE WEIGHT of catching the brazen bank robbers crushing him each day as the case dragged on. The media had dubbed the group of thieves "The Seattle Swipers" as they sought to link them to another recent unsolved bank robbery. While the Seattle Police Department denied a connection, the idea that the heists were connected made for a sexier story. And the general public bought it without giving it a second thought.

Kittrell drove toward the Seattle FC practice complex and made the mistake of turning on a Friday afternoon talk radio program. One local talk show host launched into a lengthy diatribe excoriating Seattle law enforcement for not catching the thieves after their first hit. Now one of the city's most beloved athletes was dead—and a talk show host was blaming the police.

What are these guys doing? Driving to Portland every day to pick up boxes of Voodoo Doughnuts? How come they can't catch these guys? This is getting beyond absurd.

Kittrell clicked the radio off, deciding it was better to ride in silence. And while he objected to the brash nature of the talk show hosts' characterization of the Seattle police, he agreed they should've nabbed the punks before now.

Each day that passed made it that much more difficult to locate and apprehend these men. And it made Kittrell's stomach turn. The last thing he wanted was another failure on a grand stage. He didn't know if his career could survive it, let alone his mental well-being.

Kittrell pulled into the practice complex and parked in the visitor's lot. He ambled toward the field, ignoring the security guard who had his back turned.

"Sir, I'm sorry, but this is a closed practice," the guard said as he jogged after Kittrell.

Kittrell didn't even turn around. He fished his badge out of his pocket, flashed it behind him and kept walking. "Detective Mel Kittrell, Seattle PD."

The players were huddled, listening to their coach until he dismissed them. They scattered, most of them heading toward the clubhouse. A few others lingered on the field, taking advantage of the opportunity to get in a few extra drills before joining their teammates.

Kittrell stopped short of midfield and scanned for his target.

"What are you doing out here?" came a man's voice from across the other side of the field.

Kittrell hardly paid attention to the man, who was now sprinting toward him, waving his hands in the air and squawking about how he wasn't allowed to be there.

"He's quite a character," said a man, who'd slipped up next to Kittrell unnoticed.

Startled, Kittrell turned to his right to see a reporter standing next to him.

"Cal Murphy," the man said, offering his hand to Kittrell.

Kittrell shook Cal's hand and then gestured toward the guy still running toward them. "Is he always this animated?"

"Only when you violate his rules."

"Rules?"

Cal chuckled. "Yeah, like the one that says no media is allowed on the field."

"So, he's running after you, not me?"

"It's hard to tell. He doesn't really like anyone."

Kittrell furrowed his brow. "That's strange for someone whose job is to coddle the media just to get positive stories written about the team, isn't it?"

"I don't know if I'd use the word coddle," Cal began. "But he certainly has a reputation for being the anti-media relations director."

"Well, you guys can be cruel at times."

Cal shook his head and smiled. "I will admit that there are plenty of colleagues of mine who are more interested in the click than they are the truth. Ever heard the saying, 'If it bleeds, it leads?'"

Kittrell nodded. "Unfortunately, it's a saying we repeat far too often in my line of work when a case we're working on becomes the evening's lead story."

"Well, the new mantra is more along the lines of, 'If it clicks, it sticks.'"

"At least you're being honest about what you're doing."

Cal shook his head. "That's not the kind of journalism I signed up for."

"We all sign up for something far more adventurous or exciting. But that's never what we get. You've been around long enough to know that, haven't you?"

"It doesn't mean I have to like it."

Seattle FC media relations director Paul Holloway finally reached midfield before bending over and putting his hands on his knees as he tried to catch his breath. "What ... are you two ... doing here?"

Kittrell held up his badge for Holloway to see. "I'm doing my job, just like you are, apparently."

"So am I," Cal chimed in.

"No media," Holloway said, still struggling to catch his breath. "You know … better than that, Cal … You are free to come back on Monday."

Cal shrugged and glanced at Kittrell. Kittrell gave him a sympathetic nod as he watched Cal turned and walk away.

Once Cal walked about thirty meters and was beyond earshot, Holloway stood upright and glanced at Kittrell. "That guy is nothing but trouble, always poking his nose where it doesn't belong."

Kittrell fixed his gaze on the drill taking place right in front of him, almost defiantly refusing to turn and look at Holloway in the eyes. "Cut him some slack, will ya? He's just doing his job, just like you are."

"Yeah, but—"

"It doesn't sound like you want to cut him any slack."

Holloway sighed. "Fine. You win." He paused a beat before turning to business. "What is it that you want?"

"I want to talk with a few of your players." He cut his eyes at Holloway. "Nothing to be alarmed about. Just a few routine interviews."

"Are you sure about that?"

Kittrell nodded but didn't even glance at Holloway.

"Who do you want to talk to?"

***

KITTRELL COMPLETED A FEW INTERVIEWS and lumbered back toward his car where Cal Murphy met him just outside the gate.

"You again?"

Cal laughed. "You nor Holloway will ever get rid of me that easily," he said. "You can count on that."

"Well, tell me what it is that you want. Maybe I can help—maybe not."

"Are you on the Seattle Swipers case?"

Kittrell rolled his eyes and took a deep breath.

"I'm sorry, Detective Kittrell. I'm a print journalist. The exaggerated eye roll and snarky look doesn't translate well into words. Perhaps you could say something."

"Say something, like yes or no?"

"It'd be a start."

"Fine," Kittrell said as he put his hands on his hips. "I'm on the case. There. You happy now?"

"Yes, as a matter of fact, I'm very happy because I have a few ideas I want to run by you."

"Oh, God, another gumshoe."

"No, no, no. I'm far more than that, but please just hear me out."

Kittrell sighed and threw his head back, rolling it around several times. After a moment of silence, he glanced at Cal. "Go ahead. I'm listening."

"I think this was a premeditated strike."

"Interesting theory, but right now I'm just trying to solve a robbery, not a murder."

"Who said anything about murder?"

When Kittrell looked up at Cal, he could see the reporter grinning from ear to ear.

"Are you recording this conversation?"

"Should I be?" Cal asked.

"No, you shouldn't. But I think you need to bury those conspiracy ideas."

"Yet, here you are, investigating in a strange environment."

"It was a robbery gone bad," Kittrell said, parroting the mantra his boss encouraged him to repeat.

"So, again, what are you doing out here?"

"Due diligence," Kittrell shot back.

Cal handed Kittrell a business card. "If anything comes up and you want to share it with me, here's my card. I know what it's like to work for an overbearing boss."

"But I never said anything about—"

"You didn't have to," Cal said as he strode toward his car. He stopped and turned toward Kittrell. "It was written all over your face."

Kittrell crammed the card into his shirt pocket and watched Cal drive away.

He knew exactly what it was like to work for an overbearing boss, and he hated every minute of it. Even more, he hated giving Quinn the slip just to interview a few Seattle FC players. But maybe he needed a new partner, one who could help draw out the thieves—and killers.

CHAPTER 10

CAL TRUDGED TOWARD his desk, bracing for the inevitable tongue lashing Buckman was going to give him. It wasn't as if Cal wasn't trying to do right by his editor, but he couldn't shake his hunch that Sid Westin's death wasn't merely the result of a wrong place, wrong time shooting. Yet Cal didn't have a single shred of proof, a fact he couldn't deny or excuse. Staying on this path much longer without any evidence destined him for, at best, office ridicule, or, at worst, career purgatory.

"Cal! Get in here!" Buckman bellowed.

"How does he do that?" Cal mumbled to himself. "I didn't even walk near his office."

"Buckman's got a special radar," Josh Moore offered as he looked up from his desk adjacent to Cal's. "Or he injects us all with a tracking beacon."

Cal forced a smile. He would've laughed aloud on most other days at his former college buddy's witty comment. But he knew what was coming, and he wasn't looking forward to it.

"I don't know which is more frightening."

After scanning the room, Moore looked up at Cal. "I have a special cloaking device. But it's gonna cost ya."

"I suppose you have a watch to sell me as well," Cal shot back as he gathered his papers and prepared to head toward Buckman's office.

"The watch is the cloaking device," Moore deadpanned. "Once you put it on your wrist, Buckman will never be able to locate you again. Of course, you'll be covering high school lacrosse games for the rest of your time here, but you won't be noticed by Buckman."

"There are certain assignments that just aren't worth it, no matter what," Cal said. "I can't think of anything worse than lacrosse parents."

Moore furrowed his brow. "Really? I suppose you've never dealt with Little League baseball parents then, have you?"

Cal shook his head. "I prefer not to ever find out first-hand, but I hear they are a vengeful bunch."

"We had an intern here a few years ago named Sheldon who misspelled three kids' names on one team. Buckman sent him out to cover the state tournament, and the parents from that team ate him alive. I never even saw him again. So, I'm guessing when people said he was eaten alive, they meant it in the literal sense. It's not hard to imagine those parents gnawing on Sheldon's carcass."

Cal threw his hands up in a gesture of surrender. "Okay, enough. I get the picture." He paused. "If I don't come out of Buckman's office, please come in after me."

Moore flashed a wry grin and pointed at Cal. "You got it."

Nodding in appreciation, Cal turned toward Buckman's office and slowly moved toward it. He knew exactly how Buckman would attack this particular subject.

"Sit down," Buckman barked as soon as Cal's shadow

fell across the doorway entrance. "We need to talk."

"Sure thing," Cal said. "What is it?"

"There are days I wonder why I ever hired you," Buckman said.

"Perhaps it was all my writing awards?"

Buckman chuckled to himself and gazed into the distance over Cal's shoulder. "If terms of employment here depended upon writing awards, I'd have been fired long ago. This is about something far more important."

"And what is that?" Cal said as he leaned forward.

Buckman leaned in as well and spoke more softly. "It's about your obsession with the Sid Westin case."

"Obsession? Is that what you call it?" Cal asked before taking a deep breath and preparing to stand up. "Do you have any other reason for calling me in here, other than to mock me?"

"Spoken like a reporter consumed with his story."

"I'm not consumed with anything but figuring out the truth behind what happened that day in the bank."

"What happened is fairly simple and straight forward, which is why it's so mind-boggling why you haven't been writing these stories for *The Times*."

"C'mon, Buckman, you know there's more to it than what's already out there. Just tell me with a straight face that you know it was little more than a bank robbery gone bad."

Buckman took a deep breath and appeared to look past Cal, refusing to say a word.

"If there's any doubt, I have to press on."

Buckman shook his head. "If we have a chance to break that story, I know you'll be all over it. Quite frankly, I'm not interested in transforming our sports section into a foreign tabloid. But in the meantime, I need you to write some local stories that our readers will care about."

"I don't know. This story requires some evidence before I write it and—"

"You don't have the time to get it," Buckman roared as he rose out of his seat. After he sat back down, he calmly continued, "Now, what I want you to do is to dig into this rumor that Seattle might get an NBA team again since Oklahoma City refuses to build a new arena for the Thunder."

"So Seattle is willing to build one?"

"Anything to get our Sonics back."

Before Cal could respond, his phone buzzed with a call. He glanced down at the caller ID and decided he couldn't wait another moment to answer his phone. Cal held up his index finger and eyed Buckman. "If you'll excuse me, I need to take this."

"Stay here, and put it on speaker," Buckman said. "I want to hear how you conduct your business."

"So, you're micromanaging me now?"

"Get over yourself, Cal. Put it on speaker now."

Seething, Cal answered the phone and pressed the speakerphone button. "This is Cal."

"Hey, Cal. This is Jarrett Anderson."

"Thanks for the call. It's been a while."

"Yeah, I know. Been to Mexico lately?"

Cal forced a laugh. He'd spent plenty of time trying to forget the nightmare of working with the FBI several years ago when Seahawks quarterback Noah Larson's son Jake was kidnapped and taken to Mexico until the ransom was paid. He only hoped Anderson's phone call wasn't an omen of another harrowing adventure.

"I do my best to avoid all Spanish-speaking countries these days," Cal said. "They're nothing but trouble."

Anderson chuckled. "I understand. Well, anyway, I wanted to let you know about a potential story that's brewing here."

"And you need my help?"

A moment of silence. "Okay, guilty as charged, Cal. If we could do this without you, we would. But our chief here thought you might be able to help us flush a suspect out. We don't have enough on him yet, but all we need to do is get him to make a desperate move to nail him."

"So, you're feeding me a story for the express purpose of getting him to panic?"

"Something like that."

"Well, I'm not sure my editor will go for that," Cal said. Across the desk from Cal, Buckman was wildly waving his arms and shooting evil looks at his star reporter. "I'll need to talk with him first."

"Are you out of your mind?" Buckman whispered. "Of course we want the story."

Cal sneered at him. "Don't you want me to cover the annual rumor that Seattle is getting an NBA team again?" he said in a hushed tone. "Besides, you don't even know what it is you're agreeing to."

"I don't care," Buckman said. "Tell him you can do it."

"Cal? Are you still there?" Anderson asked.

"Yep. Sorry. I'm still here." He paused. "You know, on second thought, go ahead and tell me what it is you want me to write about. I'm sure I'll be able to convince my editor to run with it. I happen to have one of the most reliable sources."

"Excellent," Anderson said as the sound of him clapping came through clearly. "Have you got a pen and paper? You're gonna want to take good notes?"

"I'm all ears."

"Great. We're nearing an indictment on Dr. Bill Lancaster. Dr. Lancaster runs a clinic in St. Louis that specializes in rehabilitation among other things. We also have record of him shipping HGH supplements to someone in your neck of the woods—and in quantities that defy logic."

"And who might that be?" Cal said, pausing from his furious note taking for a moment.

"Are you familiar with a woman named Rebecca Westin?"

CHAPTER 11

AS CAL MOVED UPSTREAM against the fans making their way to the CenturyLink Field gates, he noted the lack of buzz and excitement that usually accompanied pre-game festivities. Dour faces dominated the crowd as it marched solemnly into the stadium. Seattle FC fans had lost not only one of the team's best players, but they lost one of their favorites as well. The club's public relations team billed the game with Portland as an opportunity to celebrate Sid Westin's life as a player and as a beloved member of the city. To Cal, it looked more like a wake.

Cal made his way to his seat on press row, next to Josh Moore, who'd worked his way into *The Times*' beat writer position for Seattle FC.

Hal Presswick, who covered the Portland Timbers for The Oregonian, slapped Cal on the back as he sucked in his gut and slithered his way to his seat.

"Did you draw the short straw tonight?" Presswick said. Already sweating profusely, he wiped his forehead with the forearm of his sleeve.

"No other place I'd rather be tonight."

"You wouldn't rather be covering an NBA game? Oh, wait. Seattle doesn't have an NBA team."

Cal shook his head and smiled. "You do realize that I don't spend my spare time with my friends talking about how much better Seattle is than Portland, much less what a better sports town Seattle is either. I hate wasting time talking about facts."

Presswick dumped his laptop bag onto the desk and rolled his eyes. He slid his glasses up on his nose and sighed. Cal glanced down the row at him, waiting for Presswick's comeback. It was a fun dance the two engaged in every time they saw one another. But Presswick didn't fire off another salvo, instead choosing silence. Cal figured it must've been out of respect for the general somber mood of the press box. Almost every reporter present had dealt with Sid Westin at least once—and he was a favorite of them all. And in such a tight-knit group of writers, Westin's death had hit home hard. He wasn't just some athlete who died; he was someone they knew, someone who some of the writers might even call a friend.

Fifteen minutes before kickoff, Seattle FC played a video tribute to Westin on the jumbotron. It highlighted some of Westin's more memorable moments with the team as well as candid photos and videos of him interacting in the community. Then a moment of silence.

Though players on both teams were visibly emotional during the pre-game ceremonies, it vanished once the whistle blew to start the match. From that point on, it was just another grudge match between the Pacific Northwest's only two soccer clubs.

There were plenty of tense moments but little scoring until Matt Norfolk broke the ice. With a minute remaining until halftime, Norfolk headed in a goal on a cross from Javier Martinez to give Seattle FC a 1-0 lead.

Cal got up and took his place at the back of the line for the halftime dessert spread.

Presswick, who'd already piled a plate high of chocolate chip cookies and brownies, walked past Cal and sat down. "You're getting treated to a great match tonight. I hope you appreciate it."

"Oh, I am," Cal said. "Almost as good as an English Premiership match."

Presswick stopped and looked over the top of his glasses at Cal. "Let's not get carried away here, okay?"

Once the second half began, Portland struck back ten minutes in, tying the match on a goal from a direct kick just outside the box.

With the outcome still in doubt, the tension in the stadium grew. Cal watched fans below tense up with each buildup, trying to will their team to score or stop their opponent. It was fantastic theater, something that made almost everyone forget about the fact that Westin was gone.

As the game entered the final three minutes of stoppage time, play on the field grew more intense. The crowd seemed to hold its collective breath with each shot on goal, no matter which side of the field it occurred on.

And then, a breakthrough.

Seattle FC midfield Shawn Lynch made a nifty move on a Portland midfielder to steal the ball and streak down the field toward the Portland goal. He zipped a pass to Norfolk between two Portland defenders, and Norfolk buried the ball in the back of the net.

The crowd went crazy, celebrating as if the team had won a championship. A few fans climbed over the wall and rushed onto the field, shaking hands with Norfolk. The subsequent roundup by security officials delayed the ensuing kickoff but didn't seem to dampen the spirits of the fans. Moments after Portland kicked off, the referee blew his whistle to signal the end of the match.

Cal, who'd made his way down to the field with five minutes remaining, watched the surreal scene. It was as if all the pent up frustration and grief over Westin's death was released the moment Norfolk's shot curled neatly past the Portland goalkeeper and into the net.

"Helluva game, huh?" said Seattle FC President Fred Jameson as he raced past Cal and onto the center of the field.

Cal nodded, partially in agreement, partially in disbelief at the scene unfolding. The whole city seemed to need something to celebrate after Westin's tragic death. In some mystical way, the win served as a healing ointment, making everyone forget for just a moment about their grief and rally around a victory. To the outsider, Cal thought it would seem superficial. But it wasn't. This was a coping mechanism, a short respite from the cruel realities of a world that isn't so forgiving.

A half hour after the game ended, the players filed into the interview room to stand before a media anxious to grab a quote or a sound byte quickly enough to satisfy their tight deadlines. Seattle FC media relations director Paul Holloway grabbed a microphone and stood in the corner of the room.

"First up is Matt Norfolk," Holloway said.

Immediately, Norfolk made a brief statement. Then the questions began raining down upon him. The first few questions danced around Westin's death. It was almost as if the reporters were afraid to broach the subject out of respect for the dead. But once Holloway recognized Cal, he didn't hesitate to ask the question everybody wanted to know the answer to.

"How much did you guys talk about Sid's death tonight before the game?" Cal asked.

"A lot," Norfolk said. "Before the game began, I wanted to dedicate my play on the field tonight to Sid." He ripped his trademark wristband off and showed everyone the number 18 emblazoned on it—Sid's number. "This game tonight was for him."

Cal wasn't finished.

"Without Sid here tonight, you really picked up the slack. How much of that was adrenaline? And how much of that was you finally getting an opportunity to step out of his shadow?"

Norfolk sighed and glared at Cal. "I know you're not *The Times'* regular reporter and aren't too aware of what this team is capable of, but Sid Westin—with all due respect—wasn't the only person scoring goals on this team." He paused. "It was terrible what happened to him, and this team was much better with him on it. But am I worried about the future of this club? I think tonight's performance answered that question. We just beat the defending league champs. We're going to be just fine."

Norfolk took a few more questions before slipping through the throng of reporters.

Cal scribbled down a few notes before meandering down the hallway toward the exit. He was almost to the door when he heard a familiar voice calling his name.

"Cal!"

Cal turned around to see Javier Martinez standing in front of him.

"Javy, good to see you. Great game tonight."

Martinez ran his hand through his hair, still wet from his post-game shower. He glanced down the hallway and then looked back at Cal. "We did all right." He looked over his shoulder again. "Look, I know the Matt Norfolk angle makes for an interesting story, but if you want to know the real secret behind this team's success tonight, look at Shawn Lynch. His play at midfield is what's keeping this team together."

"Shawn's kind of new to the scene, isn't he?"

Martinez shook his head. "No, he's been around a while. But he's really come on strong lately, almost out of nowhere. I would've pegged him for a lifer on the practice squad if you would've asked me about him a year ago, but he's improved more than anyone else on the team. That's the story you're really looking for."

Cal shrugged. "Perhaps, but I'm beholden to the almighty editor for my assignments with you guys, and tonight he said to write a mood piece about Sid Westin."

"Maybe another time then, huh?"

"Sure," Cal said, firmly grabbing Martinez's shoulder. "If not me, I'll make sure Josh Moore gets on it."

Martinez sighed. "Well, I think it should be you who writes it."

"Okay, man. I didn't know you had such strong feelings about who wrote what story in the paper."

A smile spread across Martinez's lips. "Sometimes, you want the very best."

Cal chuckled and shook his head. "You're too kind, my friend. Have a good night."

Ambling across the parking lot, Cal nearly made it to his car before he felt a heavy hand laid upon his shoulder. He turned around to face Paul Holloway.

"Paul, how are you?"

Holloway glared at him.

"Okay," Cal said as he took a step back. "I take it this isn't a social call."

"You be careful out there," Holloway said, wagging his finger at Cal. "I wouldn't want you to get hurt."

"Is there something specific that I should be concerned about?"

Holloway had already turned and was walking away. "You know what you're doing out there, and you know when you cross the line. Just don't cross the line."

Cal took a deep breath and looked upward at the stars that were still bright enough to penetrate the light pollution from Seattle's evening sky. For a moment, he enjoyed the serenity. Then he collected his thoughts and climbed into his car. The peace was fleeting. He couldn't shake the sense that something dark was brooding over the team's beloved soccer club. And he wasn't going to stop digging until he learned what it was.

CHAPTER 12

LATE TUESDAY MORNING, Shawn Lynch ran passing drills with several members of the Seattle FC practice squad. Practice had ended ten minutes ago, but he still felt the need to take a few more reps before retreating to the locker room. It's not like the media members were clamoring to interview him either. Letting it all clear out was a tertiary benefit of staying out on the field.

Lynch yelled at one of the production staff members. "Where's my music?" he asked, throwing his hands in the air.

The staffer jogged toward midfield. He sat down at a table and started pushing buttons on a small soundboard there. In a matter of seconds, the sounds of Garth Brooks came blaring through the loudspeakers.

"Awww, come on, Lynch," one of the practice squad members groaned. "More country music? Geez. This is almost unbearable."

"If you can't get fired up listening to Thunder Rolls, you've got problems," Lynch fired back. "It's the perfect metaphor for a midfield that's playing well together."

The player shook his head and rolled his eyes. He turned his back on Lynch, who booted a screaming line drive pass across the field that hit the player in the back. Surprised, the player fell forward and onto the ground. He got up rubbing his back and shot Lynch a dirty look.

"I'm done for the day," he said as he glanced over his shoulder at Lynch.

Lynch laughed as he jogged toward the ball.

"I'm outta here, too," said another player.

Left alone, Lynch began juggling the ball at midfield and singing along with his favorite country music star.

The voice of a man nearby arrested Lynch's attention. "Aren't you a little young to be a fan of Garth Brooks?"

Lynch snatched the ball out of the air and stopped. He glanced to his left to see *The Times* reporter Cal Murphy standing a few feet away.

"I think the interviews are in the clubhouse," Lynch said. He turned his back on Cal and continued juggling.

Cal put his bag down on the ground and grabbed one of the balls lying nearby. He started juggling, keeping pace with Lynch.

After a few moments, Lynch stopped and cocked his head to one side. "I don't think we're having any more open try outs, but if you want to play, you should talk with coach. Now, if you'll excuse me."

Lynch started juggling again, but this time, Cal stepped in and stole the ball in midair with his foot.

Lynch put his hands on his hips. "Okay, dude, I don't know who you are, but you're starting to annoy me."

Cal stopped. "Cal Murphy from *The Times*." He offered his hand, but Lynch ignored it.

Lynch picked the ball up from the ground and tucked it under his arm. "Like I said, the interviews are taking place in the clubhouse," he said, pointing toward one of the exits.

"Yes, but the player I want to interview is right here," Cal countered. "Wanna chat for a few minutes?"

Lynch shrugged. "I must warn you that I'm not a great interview."

"Says who?"

"Says everyone."

"Well, maybe you just haven't been interviewed by the right person."

Lynch flashed a smile. "So, what's this story about that you want to write?" He gestured for Cal to sit on the front row of the small set of metal bleachers off to the side.

"You," Cal said, pulling out his notebook and digital recorder. "Well, mostly about you. A little bit about the rise of the team this season and what's behind it. But also about you."

"Where's Josh Moore? Isn't he the normal writer for you guys?"

"Yes, he's the team beat writer, but we all pitch in and help from time to time." Cal flipped a page in his notebook and then eyed Lynch closely. "So, several of your teammates have encouraged me to talk to you about how you've gone from the practice squad to the starting lineup in such a short period of time. One player even told me he would've bet you'd never have made it."

"Who said that?"

Cal chuckled. "I don't want to throw anyone under the bus."

"It was probably Martinez. He never thought much of me."

"Would it make you feel better to know that he was the one who first recommended I interview you?"

Lynch shook his head. "I don't know. He can be a snake sometimes."

"So, how'd you do it?"

"How'd I do what?"

"How did you go from perennial practice squad member to starter?"

"Lots of hard work over the past year," Lynch said. "I wasn't sure if I'd ever make it, to be honest. I was always just a little bit shy of being where I needed to be to compete and succeed at the highest level. But I changed up my training regimen—and it started to pay big dividends for me."

"What kind of things did you change?"

"Well, I stayed later than anyone else, for example. I got in the habit of hanging around so long that I became good friends with the facilities guys. They'd stick around until I left if I bought them a drink once or twice a week."

"How satisfying is it for you to finally break through here in your home town?"

"It means a lot to me," Lynch said. "It's a privilege to get to play a game that I love so much and play it in front of thousands of people each game, but I don't take it for granted, either, that I get to do it in front of the family and friends who have supported me on this journey to reach this point. Without all those people, I don't know if I ever would've made it here."

"I also heard that you just landed your first advertising gig with a local car dealership. When can we expect to see those ads start running?"

Lynch laughed. "I don't know why anyone would trust what I have to say about cars, but the dealership told me that wasn't important. What was important is that I was a home-grown celebrity."

"Are you a car person?"

"I'm a soccer person, and that's all I care about. I want to help this team win the MLS Cup and bring more pride to the Emerald City just like the Seahawks did. Having grown up here, I know what it's like to be a long-suffering fan of any pro-sports team around here, but now I have a chance to actually have a hand in changing that. I want kids to be proud to wear Seattle FC jerseys to school."

"How would you say Sid Westin's death has affected you personally?"

"Sid was an inspiration to everyone on this team. And even though he wasn't from here, I still had great respect for him. I'm sad that he's gone, but this team is going to stick together."

"Are you worried people will look at you as a beneficiary of his death?"

Lynch's eyes narrowed, and he withdrew from Cal. "Beneficiary? What are you talking about?"

"I mean, there's a big gap in the lineup now, and you're the person who will be filling it."

"Last night wasn't the first time I've started. What are you implying?"

Cal put his hands up in a gesture of surrender. "I'm not implying anything. I just noticed that you hadn't started much until John Akers got injured and you started filling in for him. He came back last night—and you likely wouldn't have started if Sid Westin was still around."

Lynch stood up. "Enough of you. Get outta here. What kind of jerk asks questions like that? I bet Paul Holloway didn't even authorize this interview. How dare you imply that I don't deserve to be starting?"

Cal stood up as well. "I'm afraid you're misinterpreting my question. That's not what I meant at all."

"Sure sounded like it," Lynch said as he sneered at Cal. "Now get lost. We're done here."

Lynch stepped back and watched Cal collect his effects and hustle away. When he was about forty yards away, Lynch dropped a ball down on the ground and kicked it in Cal's direction. After a few seconds, it smacked Cal in the head, causing him to stumble but not fall down.

Cal glanced over his shoulder at Lynch but kept walking.

"Sorry about that," Lynch said, waving at the reporter. Then he muttered under his breath. "Jerk!"

CHAPTER 13

KITTRELL RETURNED FROM LUNCH with Quinn with a new sense of urgency. Roman sent both of them a text explaining that he was convening with city council members in a closed-door meeting on Thursday afternoon about the pair of armed bank robberies in Seattle over the past few weeks. Apparently, some of the council members were concerned that the Seattle PD was failing to protect the banks, and the longer these cases went unsolved, the more it was likely to embolden thieves. In forty-eight hours, he needed some answers.

"Don't you wish you could just snap your fingers and solve cases?" Quinn asked.

"It'd make our jobs so much easier," Kittrell said as he snapped his fingers in a mocking gesture. "I swear these people must think criminals volunteer to be caught."

"It'd make our job a lot easier, too," said Darrell Barrow, one of the members of the forensics teams.

"I hope you found something," Kittrell said to Barrow. "Follow me."

Kittrell and Quinn fell in step behind Barrow as he led them down to the forensics lab. Barrow led them toward a bank of monitors, manned by Misty Morton.

"Misty, show them what you've got," Barrow said.

Morton sighed and punched a button. A snowy image appeared on the main screen. Kittrell squinted at the screen, trying to make out the figures moving around.

"Is that our perp?" Kittrell said as he leaned in and pointed at the screen.

"Supposedly," Morton said, "but he's difficult to see here."

"Can you enhance it?" Quinn asked.

"Only if you've got a time machine," Morton quipped.

Kittrell furrowed his brow and stared at her. "Come again."

"These guys were pros. They had some type of jamming device with them that makes it nearly impossible to see what exactly was going on." She leaned forward in her seat and pointed at the screen. "Now, we can tell what's going on by piecing together the eye-witness reports with the timeline you guys concocted, but I'm afraid it's never going to get much clearer than that."

"In other words, we have evidence that wouldn't be admissible in court anyway."

Morton pointed at him. "Exactly. Besides, it's not likely that you'll be able to determine anything else that happened here without a clear picture. From what it looks like, these guys stormed a bank and robbed it, shooting two men on the way out—just like we already knew. Not a single new piece of evidence was introduced here."

Kittrell rubbed his face with both hands. "There's got to be something."

"Sorry, K-man, but this is all you're gonna get," Morton said.

Kittrell eyed her closely. "K-man? Really? That's your nickname for me?"

"Beats Kitty, doesn't it?"

He growled and headed for the exit with Quinn right behind.

"I need some good news this afternoon—any good news," Kittrell said aloud.

"Then I guess you don't want to see this then?" said Pat Logan, another member of the forensics team.

Kittrell took the paper from Logan. "What's this?"

"Our report on an abandoned van found last night by a couple of officers on foot patrol," Logan said.

"And?"

"And as you can see, they pretty much wiped the van clean. We had a couple of partial prints inside the van, but they didn't match anything we had on file." Logan pointed at the page. "However, you can see that the van they found matches the description—and the license plate—of the van fleeing the scene of the bank robbery."

"So, you found the van but didn't call us?"

Logan stepped backward. "It was late. Nobody wanted to wake you for something that we weren't sure was actually what you were looking for."

Kittrell slapped Logan in the chest with the papers. "Wake me up any time for anything you find on this case. I don't care what time it is, day or night."

Logan pushed the file back toward Kittrell. "That wasn't all we found."

He returned his gaze to the report. "Did you find any bullet casings in the van?"

"Actually, we did," Logan said. He took the report from Kittrell's hands and flipped through several pages before stopping. He pointed at the bottom. "Right there."

Kittrell scanned the page, holding it up so Quinn could see as well.

"They came from a gun that was reported stolen in a

simple B and E a few months ago."

Kittrell sighed. "So, someone breaks into a home, steals this gun, and uses it in a robbery? No pawn shop stop in between."

"Nope," Logan said. "It appears that it was stolen with the expressed intent of using it in a crime. Nothing too out of the ordinary."

"Yeah," Quinn said, "except these guys are good at covering their tracks. Whoever they were, they went out of their way to keep us from looking in their direction."

"Which is why this didn't make much sense," Logan said, taking the report from Kittrell's hands and flipping a few pages. He pointed at a section of the report that showed who the van was registered to.

Kittrell whistled as he shook his head. "Now that'll blow your mind."

Quinn leaned over his shoulder again and glanced at the report. "Looks like I know who we're going to see tomorrow morning."

"What about right now?" Kittrell said.

"We've got almost two days. Besides, I've got a date with Misty Morton tonight."

Kittrell shook his head and snickered. "The gal in forensics?"

Quinn nodded.

"Whatever, man. Enjoy yourself tonight because we're going to hit it hard tomorrow."

Kittrell watched Quinn stride down the hallway. Holding the paper up again, he re-read the name. He was tempted to go without Quinn but decided against it.

Kittrell was already looking forward to the interview—and dreading it at the same time. No matter what, it was guaranteed to be interesting.

CHAPTER 14

MATT NORFOLK SAT BEHIND the glass in the Seattle FC production studio, re-reading his lines for the promotional spot set to air during the game. He loathed the endless favors the marketing department requested from him. It seemed like every campaign required his assistance. If he was honest with himself, he shouldn't have been surprised. As one of the team's emerging stars—and youngest players, too—he was definitely being positioned as the face of the franchise. Less than a week ago, it had been Sid Westin. But even before he passed away, Norfolk could tell he was being groomed to take over. Now that Sid was gone, it was obvious what the team's plan was all along.

"From the top," Joey Allman said from the other side of the glass. "We just need a little more expression from you this time. Think you can handle it?"

Norfolk nodded and read his lines again, this time drawing praise from Allman.

"Perfect! You nailed it!" Allman said. "Get on outta here so you're not late for practice."

Norfolk tossed the script in the air and hustled out of the studio and down the hall toward the locker room.

He was greeted by high fives from the team's starters,

who were almost ready to hit the field. Still wearing his sweat pants and sweat shirt, Norfolk quickly changed into his practice gear. He tugged his laces tight before tying a double knot.

"Don't tie them too tight," Javier Martinez quipped as he stopped by Norfolk's locker. "We don't need those two golden feet of yours being amputated due to lack of circulation."

Norfolk looked up at Martinez and winked. "These golden feet are going to dance right past you today out there. You better be ready."

"I'm counting on it," Martinez said before exiting the locker room and entering the field.

Norfolk took a deep breath and tried to enjoy the moment. This is what he'd worked hard for his whole life. Well, almost.

When he was younger, he wanted to play for Manchester United in the English Premier League, but that was a pipe dream even among the world's most elite soccer players. Though Manchester United was no longer the top tier team in England, it was still a team most players aspired to play for at some point in their careers. Norfolk made peace years ago that it wasn't likely to happen. It was what helped him enjoy the moment—his moment—the one that had him leading Seattle FC to the top of the league standings in Major League Soccer.

He'd worked hard to reach this point in his career where he'd emerged as the team's top goal scorer and face of the franchise. He was done taking lip from anyone. This was his team now, and he was ready to lead them to a title.

Norfolk glanced at himself in the mirror one more time before running onto the field. However, he didn't make it out of the tunnel before Tim Peterson slid in front of him.

"What are you doing?" Norfolk asked. "Get outta my way."

"We need to talk," Peterson said.

"About what?"

"Everybody on this team is getting pretty sick and tired of you acting like your stuff doesn't stink," Peterson began. "We're all out here working our tails off to make this team better—not just you. And the guys would appreciate it if you'd be a little more gracious in your postgame interviews."

"You're crazy, man." Norfolk tried to walk past Peterson, but Norfolk blocked his way.

"No, I'm not. The team sent me to talk to you today. We're all sick of it. This isn't your team. This is our team. And we'd appreciate the common courtesy of extending some recognition to us."

"I never hog the limelight."

"That's not what it sounded like on Monday. To the uninitiated, it sounded like you're the sole reason this team is in first place—and like Sid's death didn't mean much of anything."

"That's a horrible interpretation of what I said."

Peterson shrugged. "Maybe, but that's how it came across. And we want it to stop."

Norfolk rolled his eyes and shoulder-checked Peterson, pushing his way past..

"Not cool, man."

"How's this for not cool?" Norfolk said as he spun around and punched Peterson in the face.

Peterson staggered around for a moment before crashing to the ground, holding his head just seconds after Norfolk hit him.

"Now stop being a jerk and tell all your jealous pals to get over it. And if they've got a problem, they can come see me directly," Norfolk barked over Peterson.

Norfolk turned and jogged out of the tunnel toward the field. He never even saw the reporter from the local radio station standing a few feet away and capturing the entire exchange on his phone.

CHAPTER 15

KITTRELL SHOVED A COFFEE CUP into Quinn's hands before he made it to his desk. "Don't even sit down. You know where we're headed."

Quinn smiled and thanked Kittrell for the coffee before taking a sip.

"I take it your date went well last night," Kittrell said as he pushed open the glass doors and exited the precinct.

"She was something else. Let me tell you."

"I'd rather you not."

Kittrell unlocked the car with his fob, and both detectives climbed inside. He waited until Quinn was settled inside before putting the keys in the ignition. "You ready for this?"

Quinn laughed. "Of course. I was born ready."

"This ought to be interesting," Kittrell said as he turned the key and the engine roared to life.

Quinn turned on the radio and started to scan the AM band for stations.

"Really? Talk radio?" Kittrell said.

"Beats listening to techno pop with vapid lyrics."

Kittrell nodded. "You've got a point there."

Quinn went through a half-dozen stations until he landed on KJR's Mitch in the Morning. Mitch Levy and his crew were dissecting the recent posting of a video between a pair of Seattle FC players getting into it.

"I love to see this kind of passion from players," Mitch said. "And Norfolk is right. These guys need to quit getting their panties in a bunch and stop being so sensitive. Norfolk is leading this team, and he was doing it before, God rest his soul, Sid Westin was killed. But let's get to today's really juicy news and talk about—"

Kittrell turned the radio off. "I'd rather listen to silence than that."

"You know we're going to catch these guys, whoever they are," Quinn said.

"I know. I just—"

"Hey, this isn't going to be the Arnold Grayson case all over again. You gotta believe that."

Kittrell nodded. "I hope you're right. But it's about to get real interesting."

He slowed as he turned onto a usually quiet street that today was teeming with news vans and reporters.

"What's all this?" Quinn asked.

"Journalism in the twenty-first century."

A photographer rushed over toward the detectives' car and snapped a picture of Quinn, who shielded his face with his hands. Kittrell served notice to the reporters to clear a path by revving his engines. A few straggling reporters darted out of the way once they turned around, apparently pleased to see a pair of detectives pulling into the driveway of the house they'd staked out.

"Whether anything happens today or not, at least these poor, miserable souls have a story for tomorrow," Kittrell said.

Quinn snickered and threw a piece of gum in his mouth.

He held out the pack to Kittrell. "Wanna piece?"

Kittrell shook his head. "But I'd like to give them a piece of my mind."

"Don't make this any more difficult than it's already going to be."

Moments later, the two detectives were standing in front of the door to the Westins' house.

"Does Rebecca know we're coming?" Quinn asked.

"I didn't tell her, if that's what you mean."

"On purpose?"

"You ought to know me by now. I prefer to surprise people. I get far better reactions, reactions that tell the truth about what a person is thinking or feeling, not a well-measured response."

Kittrell rang the doorbell.

A few seconds later, the airy voice of a woman drifted from the other side of the door. "Please go away. We're not interested in talking."

"Mrs. Westin, my name is Mel Kittrell, and I'm a detective with the Seattle PD. We're following up with you for a few questions regarding your husband's death."

The door slowly swung open, and the detectives entered amid a flurry of cameras clicking behind them. Quinn leaned against the door to close it shut once he was all the way inside. Rebecca Westin turned the deadbolt and gestured for them to enter the living room just off the main entryway.

"This is a nice place you have here, Mrs. Westin," Kittrell said.

"Please, call me Rebecca," she said. "And thanks." She paused. "Can you tell me what this is all about? Have you found the killers?"

Kittrell glanced at her hands, which she wrung several

times before she took a seat on a small couch to the right of a larger couch. The detectives sat on the larger couch.

"Did somebody knock, Becs? I heard—" A man appeared from around the corner, wearing a towel. His hair appeared wet. "Oh, I'm sorry."

Kittrell glanced at Rebecca, who'd put her head down and was shielding her eyes with her right hand. He then stood up and offered his hand. "Detective Mel Kittrell with the Seattle PD. And you are?"

"Wet," the man said. He wiped his hand off on his towel. "Jonathan Umbert, Sid Westin's agent."

Quinn stood up and shook the man's hand as well before sitting back down.

"Would you care to join us?" Kittrell said before he sat down.

Putting up both hands in a gesture of surrender, Umbert declined. "I don't want to intrude. Besides, I need to finish getting ready."

"Just go, Jonathan," Rebecca finally said.

"Nice to meet you," Umbert said before he scurried down the hall.

"I apologize, Detectives. He stopped by to check in on me after his racquetball game at the gym this morning, and he had an emergency meeting suddenly scheduled that he needed to get ready for but didn't have enough time. I told him he could shower here so he could make it in time."

"We're not here to judge, Rebecca," Kittrell said. He glanced at Quinn with a knowing look.

Quinn leaned forward. "But we do have a few questions for you."

Rebecca turned over the newspaper that had been lying on the coffee table. "Okay, I'm happy to help however I can, especially if it'll help catch the men who murdered my husband."

"There have been quite a few interesting developments in the case lately, but I first want to begin by asking you about the state of your marriage. I know better than to believe everything I read in the papers, so I thought it would be best to get the answer straight from you."

"I appreciate that, Detective. It wasn't nearly as bad as the media made it out to be." She clasped her hands together and gazed out the window for a moment before continuing, "It wasn't perfect, but it wasn't horrible. We had our issues like all married couples, but I'd say we got along quite peachy."

"That's good to hear," Quinn chimed in.

"Yes, it certainly wasn't the house of horrors the papers made it sound like it was. Is that why you stopped by? To find out about my marriage?"

Kittrell shook his head. "Actually, we stopped by for a different reason."

"Oh? What's that?"

"It's about the van used in the robbery," Kittrell said. "We were able to track it down a couple of days ago." He eyed her cautiously, hoping to spot an expression or gesture that might give her away. Still nothing. "It was registered to your husband."

"Sid had a van?" she asked incredulously. "If he did, he neither told me about it, nor did he ever show it to me. Are you sure?"

"It's registered in his name right here," Quinn said as he pulled out a copy from a file folder he was holding. He set it down on the table and pointed at Sid's name.

"Where would he have kept it?" Rebecca wondered aloud.

"We were hoping you could help us with that, ma'am," Kittrell said. "Did you have a weekend home on the water somewhere or a mountain cabin?"

She nodded. "We have a cabin in the mountains just northwest of Port Angeles, but I would've seen it there."

Kittrell kept peppering her with questions. "A storage unit perhaps?"

"Not that I'm aware of."

"Did you store a boat anywhere?"

"Yes, we did have a boat that he kept at Eagle Harbor on Bainbridge Island, but I don't know of any storage space there where he would've been able to keep such a vehicle."

"I know the place," Quinn said as he stood up. "We'll go check it out."

Kittrell stood up as well and looked at the widow, who struggled to put forth a believable performance that she was indeed struggling with Sid's death. "Look, I know this may be difficult for you as people sift through your life—especially the press—but I can assure you that we'll be discreet about how we share information publicly. We'll do our best not to blindside you."

"Thank you, Detective Kittrell," she said, shaking his hand. "I appreciate that."

"Ma'am," Quinn said, nodding at her before heading toward the front door.

Kittrell lingered behind for a moment. "And if there's anything else you want to tell us or feel like would help with our investigation, don't hesitate to call me," he said, slipping his business card into her hand. "From the appearance of things, this looks like a bank robbery gone bad, but this latest information about the van used by the thieves being registered in your husband's name does make us want to take a deeper look at this. We're not trying to stick our noses where they don't belong, but we want answers just like you do."

"Thank you," she said, sniffling as she looked down.

Kittrell acted as though he was done, but he wasn't. He took a deep breath as he initiated a tactic to draw what psychologists referred to as "door knob confessions." But with his own twist. Patients often divulge the most pertinent information in a counseling session just moments before heading out the door. And while Kittrell wasn't in a counseling session, he was tinkering with human psychology. He'd been a detective long enough to know that closing cases consisted of good work and oftentimes a bit of luck. And sometimes it was necessary to set a trap, panic the suspect, and collect the bounty—all part of his inventive door knob confession tactic.

"Didn't you have a break-in a few months ago?" he said as he grabbed the handle to the front door.

She nodded. "Yeah. Why?"

"Well, I found it interesting that some of the bullets found at the scene of the bank robbery matched the markings of a bullet fired from your husband's gun."

Rebecca furrowed her brow. "How would you know that?"

"When he registered his gun, he fired a bullet and gave it to us just in case we ever needed it. It's quite the coincidence, don't you say?"

She shook her head. "I—I don't really know what to say."

"Your husband certainly didn't come across as an avid fan of guns. But apparently he was. Looks like he was also skilled at keeping secrets."

"I think it's time for you to leave, Detective."

"Perhaps you were more skilled than he was."

"Thank you, Detective. I've already had a trying enough morning with all the media reports swirling around about me. I'm not in the mood to take on more accusations. That will be all," she said as she grabbed the door and started to close it.

Kittrell stumbled outside in front of the gawking news media members, who captured the entire incident on film.

"What was that all about?" Quinn said discreetly.

"I just gave Mrs. Rebecca Westin reason to panic."

"In the vain of the late great Sid Westin, 'You cheeky little devil.'"

Kittrell suppressed a smile and headed toward their car. He didn't want to give the media anything else to talk about. "Did you see this morning's paper?"

Quinn nodded. "Can't believe you're just now bringing this up. It would've been far more interesting than driving over here in silence—or listening to Mitch in the Mornings."

"We need to get a paper."

Quinn held up a copy he'd snagged on his way out of his apartment earlier that morning. "No need. We've got everything we need right here."

CHAPTER 16

CAL SHUFFLED INTO THE OFFICE in time to make *The Times*' sports department's daily 3:30 PM budget meeting. The meeting consisted of an unscientific approach to culling out all the day's news that wouldn't be of interest to the majority of the Seattle area readers. Unlike some areas of the country where Cal had lived, Seattle sports fans were far more passionate about their teams than they were about the national perspective of a particular sport. If fans cared about the NFL, they only cared about the news coming out of the league office if it had anything to do with their beloved Seahawks. Major League Soccer fans wanted to know about Seattle FC, but nothing more. Baseball was the same way: If there was no Mariners' news, the majority of fans didn't care.

But everyone cared about local celebrities and socialites. It's why Cal's story from the night before found its way not to the front of the sports section but to the front page of the entire paper.

FBI Tracks PED Ring to Seattle; Eyes Late Soccer Star's Wife read the headline emblazoned across the top of the paper.

Cal adroitly wrote the piece based off the information given him in a way that cast suspicion on Rebecca Westin but protected the paper from any frivolous lawsuits. His article revealed that the FBI was investigating a performance-enhancing drug connection between Dr. Bill Lancaster, a doctor located in St. Louis, and Rebecca Westin. Cal's FBI agent contact went on the record as a source and revealed that Rebecca was being investigated for being a distributor for Dr. Lancaster's illegal activities. Reluctantly, Cal wrote the story. He'd expressed hesitation to involve himself in the reporting to Buckman fearing that he might compromise his current assignment. Buckman shrugged it off by saying that if any of his reporters were going to be digging around on this case, he wanted his star reporter doing it—even if there were two fantastic stories happening simultaneously.

Cal couldn't help but feel like perhaps the two were connected in some strange way, but he didn't possess a shred of proof.

Shifting in his seat, he looked at Josh Moore, who'd just slumped into his chair. Cal tried to get a read on his colleague and friend. "How was the funeral this morning?"

Moore sighed. "It was a funeral. Lots of people talking about how awesome Sid was. I always hate going to funerals for people I didn't know very well because it makes me wish I had gotten to know them."

"It still beats going to funerals of people you do know."

"Not if they're people I never liked."

"Good point."

"Listen, I wish you'd give me a heads up about these stories," Moore said.

Cal tapped his pen on his pad and stared out the window of the conference room. "I didn't want to write it at all, but Buckman insisted upon it."

"Either way, it makes my life more difficult."

Standing at the doorway, fellow sports writer Eddie Ramsey sighed loudly, drawing both Cal's and Moore's attention. "Cal is always making everyone's life difficult," Ramsey said as he sauntered into the room. "But he's going to get his comeuppance soon enough. You can only live for so long on a reputation built ages ago. At some point, people are going to ask, 'What have you done for me lately?' And then they'll look at Cal and realize the answer is nothing."

"Somebody's off his meds this morning," Cal quipped.

Ramsey pulled out the chair next to Cal and sat down. "Cal, Cal, Cal—the guy who doesn't realize that everybody else hates him because he's a fraud."

Cal clenched his fists and prepared a witty comeback before deciding against it. Ramsey liked to get under his skin, which Cal assumed to be little more than professional jealousy. He hated that Ramsey's comments bothered him more than they should have. Cal knew he should have ignored the petty quips and caustic cut downs, but he couldn't. Instead, Cal spent time brooding over them.

Other staff reporters wandered into the room, filling up the chairs until Buckman finally walked in five minutes past the hour. He hated to wait for anyone and had made a practice out of being late so as to be the final person to show up at a meeting.

"Are we ready to begin?" Buckman asked as he collected a stack of papers on the conference room table.

A few half-hearted nods signaled to Buckman that he was in control of the room and could begin whenever he pleased.

"Very well then," he began. "I want to talk about today's paper before we get into what's on tap for tomorrow."

Cal pushed his chair back a couple of feet and sighed.

"Here we go again," he muttered under his breath to Moore.

"Nice of you to join us today, Cal," Buckman said. "But I want to start with you."

"What did I do now?"

"It's what you didn't do that has me pretty upset right now."

Cal scrunched up his face and stared at Buckman. "Okay. Would you mind elaborating?"

"Perfect," Buckman said. "That face you made right there. Don't move. I want everyone to look at you."

Cal tried to hold the awkward expression so the rest of the people around the table could observe the big mistake he was apparently making—though he wasn't sure what Buckman was talking about.

Buckman snapped his fingers. "Exactly. Don't you move, Cal." He turned toward everyone else. "That look right there—it shows contempt."

"Contempt?" Cal said. "Annoyance maybe, but not—"

Buckman wagged his finger at Cal. "No, no, no. Keep your mouth shut. We don't need you to interject any comments. We just need that expression on your face."

"But I didn't do anything," Cal protested.

"Yet, you did—with one look." Buckman looked at everyone else in the room. "Do you see what he's doing? Do you see how his mouth is turned down and his brow is furrowed? It's apparent that he's not aligned with me here."

"Come on, I—"

"And that's why you lost your press credentials at Seattle FC today."

"What?" Cal said, pushing his chair back from the table. "You've gotta be kidding me."

"I wish I was, Cal. But you are done." Buckman turned

and looked at the rest of the reporters. "You see, it doesn't matter how many awards you've won, if you continue to skirt the rules, eventually it will catch up with you."

"That's not fair.".

"Fair or not, it's accurate—and it's the truth. You know good and well that you've been toeing a fine line over the past few days. Now it all caught up with you."

"This is absurd."

Buckman narrowed his eyes. "You're the reporter I most wanted on this story, but Seattle FC scuttled that when they revoked your credentials."

"I didn't do anything wrong. I just reported the news."

"But you didn't abide by their policies. You thumbed your nose at them and did what you wanted."

"Are you listening to me? I didn't do anything wrong."

"Then why are you out in the cold, blacklisted by the club? Answer me that. Besides, it's too late now. Ramsey is taking over the story. I've got some other assignments for you that we'll discuss later."

Cal furrowed his brow and leaned on the table. "I wrote the story that you insisted I write."

Buckman glared at him. "Why don't you leave the room so we can finish our meeting? You don't have anything for tomorrow's paper anyway."

"I hear there's a big high school swim meet downtown this weekend, Cal," Ramsey said with a wink. "It's got your name all over it."

"Shut up, Ramsey," Buckman growled.

Cal collected his papers and left. He didn't mind getting chewed out by Buckman, most of the time it made him a better reporter, but he hated being treated unfairly. Despite his protests, Cal was forced to write the story about Rebecca

Westin—and he knew that was ultimately why Seattle FC brass was upset. It had nothing to do with him finding creative ways to get interviews out of players. And Buckman knew it too, no matter what he said in the conference room in front of all the other reporters.

Cal sat down and opened his Twitter account on his desktop. He knew it was against his better judgment—as well as against his personal policy of never reading the comments. But there was no other assignment he had looming over him. Once the web page opened, he started to scan the comments. They were cruel—and terrifying. Death threats, unfounded accusations. It was an all-out assault on his integrity as a journalist as well as his manhood. While he contemplated replying, he concluded there was nothing he could say that would assuage the attackers. They were out for blood and gleefully circled him in the digital waters.

Without an outlet to write about what he'd learned, Cal slumped in his chair. He threw a pen at his monitor and sighed. Instead of fighting for Cal, Buckman had caved to the pressures of an organization that had grown more powerful in recent months—at least that was Cal's assessment. He adored Buckman, but he had a distinct difference of opinion in this situation. Yet Cal wondered if he'd be able to re-establish his reputation before it was too late.

CHAPTER 17

EARLY THURSDAY MORNING, Kittrell arrived at the Seattle Police Department headquarters to review some of his notes from the case. He'd tried not to fret about the deadline Chief Roman had imposed upon them to find something that would assuage the city council members he was scheduled to meet with later that afternoon. But with daylight just breaking across the bay and Kittrell already at his desk, it was obvious he'd succumbed to worry.

And so had Quinn.

"Looks like we both had the same idea," Quinn said, setting down a cup of coffee next to Kittrell's stack of reports.

"Thanks," Kittrell said, reaching for the cup but refusing to take his eyes off the report in front of him.

"What's so interesting there?"

Kittrell continued to scan the page without responding.

"Hey, earth to Kittrell. You still with us, buddy?"

Kittrell looked up at Quinn. "Sorry, just trying to figure out if we missed something."

"You may not have missed something, but we found something," came a voice from across the room.

They both turned around to see Darrell Barrow from the forensics lab striding toward them.

"Gentlemen, I think we found something you're gonna wanna see."

Kittrell scrambled to his feet and followed Barrow and Quinn back toward the lab.

"What did you find?" Kittrell said as they entered the room.

Misty Morton was furiously typing on her keyboard but paused and spun around in her chair, pointing toward the large monitor on the wall. She glanced at Quinn and shot him a dirty look, a moment that didn't escape Kittrell.

"It looks like we have our first suspect," Barrow said.

Quinn and Kittrell both stared at the screen.

"Who's Wayne Geller?" Quinn asked as he studied the picture and details of the rap sheet of the man whose image was now larger than life on the monitor. He didn't look menacing—and neither did his prior arrests, which were nothing more than a few speeding tickets and misdemeanor charges like public drunkenness and disorderly conduct.

Morton stood up and began to pace next to the monitor. "When we first went through the van dusting for fingerprints, we didn't find any—not even those of Sid Westin. But we forgot to dust the gas cap. And when we did, we captured Geller's prints. They were the only prints in or on the entire vehicle."

"Doesn't look like our typical armed robber, but let's bring him in," Kittrell said.

***

KITTRELL WAS GRATEFUL apprehending Geller wasn't a messy ordeal. He and Quinn both hated chasing down suspects. The suspects never got away, but they almost always tried—the great misfortune of having two detectives who'd medaled in the state high school track and field 100-meter dash come for them. Geller, who worked at a body shop just outside of downtown, insisted it was all a big mistake, and to prove it he'd be more than willing to talk with them at the precinct. Kittrell decided against sticking handcuffs on a man who was so compliant, despite Quinn's protests.

To Kittrell, Geller didn't quite look the part of an armed robber. He was clean cut, polite, and well spoken. All of his responses to Kittrell's questions didn't seem rehearsed but authentic and calmly answered. After a half hour, Kittrell announced that they needed to take a break and they'd resume in a few minutes. Quinn followed him out of the interview room.

"Is this our guy?" Roman asked as he wandered up on the detectives.

Quinn shook his head.

"Kittrell?" Roman said, turning to look at him.

"I-I don't know. It doesn't look like it."

"But his prints were found on the van?"

"Yes, on the gas cap, which he said came from when he did work on the van and filled it up as a courtesy for the customer."

"What about his alibi?"

"He claims he was at work that morning."

Morton walked up and handed a folder to Kittrell. He couldn't help but notice again how she ignored Quinn. "K-Man, you might wanna take a look at these before you start buying everything this Geller guy says."

"What's this?" Kittrell said as he opened the folder.

"Cell phone records for Geller," Morton said. "And I was able to triangulate his location during the time of the robbery based off a text he sent."

"And?"

"He was there, no doubt about it," she said. She turned and started to walk away down the hall. "Thank me later with a drink, K-Man."

Roman smiled. "Go nail him, guys. Make me forget about Arnold Grayson."

Kittrell waited until Roman was out of earshot before he moved. "I could forget about Arnold Grayson if Chief would stop reminding me."

"Ditto that."

The detectives re-entered the room with Geller. Kittrell sat down across from his suspect while Quinn remained standing in the corner.

"So, Mr. Geller, some new evidence has come to light about your whereabouts during the time of the robbery. It appears as though you weren't at your garage working as you claim but indeed were at the Puget Sound Bank downtown branch where the robbery occurred."

Geller didn't flinch. "I think I'll speak with my lawyer now."

***

KITTRELL AND QUINN RETURNED from lunch to find Geller in the interview room with his lawyer. During their break, the detectives spoke with the district attorney about offering Geller a plea deal. Based on video evidence, they were able to identify Geller and determine that he wasn't the one who shot and killed Westin and the security guard. And that was the suspect Chief Roman wanted more than anyone.

"So, Mr. Geller, let's pick up where we left off. We know

DEAD DROP | 115

you were at the robbery, but what we'd rather know is who was with you."

Geller's lawyer put his hand on Geller's chest. "You don't have to answer that."

Kittrell studied Geller closely and watched sweat bead up on his forehead. "Of course you don't have to answer it. But, if you don't, the consequences could be dire."

"Wha-what are you talking about?"

"Dire, Mr. Geller," Quinn said as he stepped forward and leaned on the table. "As in serious time in lock up." He paused and walked back into the corner of the room before he turned around again. "Like, you might miss your five-year-old daughter's graduation from high school kind of dire. Getting a conviction for armed robbery and accomplice to murder ought to be easy enough."

"They're just trying to intimidate you," Geller's lawyer said. "You don't have to say anything."

Kittrell and Quinn remained quiet, choosing to let Geller squirm until he acquiesced.

Wait for it. Wait for it.

"What kind of deal are we talking about?" Geller said.

Kittrell slid a folder to Geller's lawyer. "One I think you'll be pleased with."

The lawyer scanned the terms of the agreement and nodded approvingly.

"There is one catch: You're gonna have to cooperate," Quinn said.

Geller looked at his lawyer again. "If you did it," the lawyer said, "sign it. You're not going to get a better deal than this."

Geller hesitated. "He'll kill me, you know."

"So you feel like your choices are either to rot in prison

or die a free man?" Kittrell said. "I know which one I'd pick—because if this guy is as dangerous as you think, he can get to you in prison as well."

Geller picked up the pen and scribbled his name on the bottom line.

Kittrell reached across the table and dragged the document back toward him. "Thank you, Mr. Geller. We'll get started in the morning." Kittrell looked at the lawyer. "Say, nine o'clock?"

The lawyer nodded.

"Very well. Nine o'clock it is," Kittrell said. He stood up and looked at Geller. "You made a bad decision a few days ago, but today you made a good decision. It's how you get on track to putting your life back together. You won't regret this."

The detectives entered the hallway and were greeted by Chief Roman, who wore an exuberant expression. "Did he agree to work with us?"

Quinn nodded.

"Outstanding! This will make my meeting with city council so much more enjoyable this afternoon," Roman said before hustling off down the hall.

***

PEYTON TUCKER KISSED HIS ROSARY and glanced down the hallway once more. He said a quick prayer and lumbered toward his target. With each step, he descended deeper into the depths of regret. He knew he could turn around at any moment and save himself. His soul could still be saved. He reached down and kissed his rosary again.

Not that it mattered. Any display of faith he made was about to be obliterated by his actions. He wondered how he ended up here, in the King County Jail on this night. How did someone know his darkest secrets, his moments of grave indiscretion? It was like he was targeted. But it did no good to ponder such things now. He'd manage the guilt somehow. It'd be far easier than dealing with the consequences of losing those closest to him or the shame he might endure. It was just one simple task.

Tucker slowed his gait and glanced over his shoulder once more. He needed to make sure there would never be any record of what he was about to do. The security cameras panned toward him, and he took a small step backward to avoid being captured. He waited until the oscillating mechanism moved away again, then he dashed toward the nearest cell, the one that contained Wayne Geller.

Geller slept peacefully on his cot. He didn't stir when Tucker opened the cell door. He didn't flinch when Tucker slipped a pair of handcuffs on each wrist either, tethering him to the metal bed frame.

Tucker looked skyward once more and muttered a prayer. Father, forgive me for what I'm about to do.

He knew it went against the teachings of the Catholic church. Forgiveness was bestowed after you did something, often over a sin committed in a moment of weakness. But the mistakes Tucker had made long ago—and had never been absolved for—was why he was standing over the sleeping body of Wayne Geller. Tucker's past had caught up with him in the most unlikely way, but absolution would only come through commission of another sinful act—one of the worst acts of all.

Tucker grabbed the pillow from the empty top bunk and took a deep breath. If he was going to get away with this, he needed everything to be executed to perfection.

He gripped the pillow on each end and slipped it on top of Geller. Tucker then placed his knee on Geller's chest, forcing his entire weight on his victim.

For a moment, nothing. Then Geller began to move. He tried to thrash violently but couldn't. He couldn't move, smothered by Tucker's six-foot-three, 300-pound frame. Only the slight clinking of the handcuff chains on the bed frame interrupted the silence in the dark. It didn't take too long for Geller to lose consciousness.

Tucker then worked quickly to wrap Geller's bed sheet around his neck and hoist him up, hanging him from the ceiling. Given what had happened to Geller earlier in the day, Tucker doubted anyone would look into his death any further. By this time tomorrow, Geller's life would be nothing more than the story of a sad and frightened criminal who saw no other way out.

He double-checked his knots and gathered his cuffs. Careful not to make any noise or get caught on camera, Tucker eased open the cell door and waited until the camera swept past him and focused on the opposite direction. He shut the cell door behind him and slipped into the hallway and out of the back door.

Five minutes after he returned to his post, his shift ended. He said good night to several other officers and got into his truck to head home. After buckling up, he hung his rosary beads over his rearview mirror and turned the ignition.

Despite his best efforts to compartmentalize what he'd just done, Tucker couldn't. The image of a squirming Geller was burned into the recesses of his mind. He was so consumed with his guilt that he never saw the dump truck hurtling toward him as he eased onto the gas pedal.

CHAPTER 18

CAL DIALED KELLY'S NUMBER on his cell phone as he sipped his morning coffee. He usually spent his Friday mornings at home, preparing for a late night of sports coverage. Seattle always seemed to have some marquee event scheduled for Friday nights, a fact that more often than not disappointed his wife, Kelly. She preferred to have Cal all to herself on the eve of the weekend, yet no matter how many times he explained that working on Friday nights and weekends was the life of a sports writer, she still complained about it. But tonight his schedule was free, along with the rest of his day.

"What are you covering tonight, hon?" Kelly asked.

"I've actually got the night off."

"What? And you let me go out of town? Cal Murphy, I swear if you—"

"It wasn't by choice."

Kelly stopped her rant and turned sympathetic. "What happened?"

"Buckman pulled me off the Sid Westin story."

"Why would he do that?"

"This story is getting a little crazy right now. But long story short, Buckman is catching heat for a story he asked me to write so he's got to look tough. Paul Holloway, the media relations guy for Seattle FC, didn't appreciate how I conducted some of my interviews and called the paper to complain about me. So, Buckman's using Holloway's complaint as the reason why he's handed the story over to someone else—but I know better."

"Buckman's trying to save his own skin."

"I don't blame him. He made a show of everything in front of the staff yesterday, but I don't think that's how he really feels. He's just trying to do what management wants him to do."

"So what are you gonna do?"

"Probably cover that Red Bull boat race on Sunday."

"Well, who's handling the Sid Westin story?"

"Take a wild guess."

"It better not be Eddie Ramsey."

Cal dropped into his sarcastic voice. "I know he's your favorite, so try to contain your joy."

"Any time a guy pukes on you at an office Christmas party, he's forever deemed a loser—and I'll never forgive him."

"At least he didn't get any on your shoes."

Kelly groaned. "You're too much. That's one memory I'd love to purge from my mind. If I try hard enough to recall that evening, I can still smell his puke."

"Well, the story is in capable hands now," Cal said again.

"Your sarcasm is rich here."

"What? I mean just because Ramsey botched up his interview with the mayor's wife about her initiative to increase tennis in the inner city. that doesn't mean he'll make similar mistakes here. It's not like once you call the mayor's wife "sir" multiple times even after she's corrected you—and continues correcting you—you can just shrug it off as a bad day. Forget the fact that the mayor's wife wrote in her memoir before Ramsey interviewed her that she was mocked as a child for having a boy face. There was no need for her to be so sensitive about it. I'm sure it was all just a big misunderstanding."

"Nothing left for you to do but enjoy your day off."

Cal sighed. "I suppose, but I was having too much fun looking into the story."

"You are one twisted man."

"I'll take that as a compliment." He paused. "Speaking of having fun, how are you and Maddie doing?"

"We're having a wonderful time. It's simply beautiful here."

"What about things with your mom."

She took a deep breath. "It's simply beautiful here."

"Okay. I get it. Have fun and kiss Maddie for me."

"Oh, you know us," she said.

Cal's phone buzzed with a message. "Yeah, yeah," he said before trying to open the message from a number he didn't recognize.

"Cal, are you still listening?"

"Sorry, Kelly. I just got a text message."

"Which is obviously more important than anything I have to say."

"It's not that. It's just that . . . ." Cal trailed off as he began to look more closely at the message he'd just received and the attachment that came along with it.

Kelly waited for a few moments before trying to get his attention. "Cal? Cal? Are you still there?"

"Yes, honey, I'm still here."

"No, I mean are you still present in this conversation?"

"Uh, huh."

"What is it, Cal? I know you're not paying attention any more."

Cal scanned the images attached in the text message, which happened to be pictures of a document. He took too long to answer her.

"That's fine, Kelly."

"Cal? You're answering questions I didn't ask. What are you doing?"

He came out of his fog and caught the tail end of her question. "What was that again?"

"I know you're not paying attention to me. All I said was—"

Cal took a deep breath. "I'm sorry. I just got an interesting text message."

"Which you had to read immediately, of course."

"Of course."

She sighed. "Well, don't keep me in suspense any longer. What did it say?"

"It was a copy of the divorce papers Sid Westin served to his wife the day he was killed."

"Some people just don't know how to handle a break up, do they?"

"You joke, but this is serious."

"Cal, do you honestly think this could possibly be related to his death? Sounds like a click-bait tweet on Twitter as opposed to a piece of the puzzle surrounding his death—if there even if a puzzle."

"You might be right, but I need to check this out."

"And how are you gonna do that now that Buckman has pulled you off the story—and most likely Rebecca Westin thinks you're a low life for writing that story about her?"

"I have my ways."

Cal hung up, and his phone buzzed again with another message. This time, it was a series of photos.

***

AN HOUR AND A HALF LATER, Cal stood at the back-door entrance of Rebecca Westin's house. He'd hopped the fence surrounding her backyard and hoped that she'd find him harmless enough to let in. Cal was banking on the fact that while she may have hated a "Cal Murphy" who wrote for *The Times*, she wouldn't recognize him if he walked through her front door—or back door.

He waited patiently for someone to come to the door. When she peered through the blinds at him, he pushed his faux glasses up on his nose and waved at her. His Eddie Ramsey impersonation at office parties had become legendary—and now it was time to put it to use for a good cause.

Rebecca cracked the door open. "May I help you?"

"Mrs. Rebecca Westin?"

"Yes?"

"I'm Eddie Ramsey from *The Times*, and I wanted to talk with you for a few moments if you wouldn't mind. It's about your late husband."

She hesitated for a moment and then swung the door open. "As long as your name isn't Cal Murphy, I guess I'm okay with it. I need to get my side of the story out."

Cal laughed and even included the classic Ramsey snort. "Oh, Cal's not such a bad guy. He was just doing what he was told."

"Writing an article about me like that just days after my

husband was killed in a bank robbery is about the least tasteful thing anyone could've done to me. I can hardly believe any editor would assign such a story—never mind the fact that it isn't true."

"Well, we only write what our editor tells us to write, Mrs. Westin."

"So, you're a bunch of mindless robots?" She raised her eyebrows before walking slowly toward the living room.

"I wouldn't say that's a fair characterization. Perhaps of Cal Murphy, but not anyone else."

She turned around. "I knew I'd like you." She gestured toward the couch. "Please, have a seat."

Cal sat down and pulled out his notebook. "Thank you, Mrs. Westin."

"Please, call me Rebecca."

"Okay, Rebecca. I hope you don't find my line of questioning insensitive either, but there's something I wanted to ask you about, and I don't want to make a public spectacle of it."

"Is that why you came to the back door?"

He nodded. "The news crews can be cruel at times in the way they capture your every move."

"Not to mention overbearing."

"That, too. And it's why I wanted to ask you these questions discreetly. I hope you don't find them as too invasive either."

"Depends on what it's about."

Cal took a deep breath. "Someone sent us some documents today regarding your relationship with your late husband."

"Oh?"

"Yes. They were divorce papers dated the day of Sid's

death. And according to the person who sent them to our office, they were served to you on that same day. Can you verify that for me?"

"First, Cal Murphy. Now, you. Geez, you people are relentless. What does this even have to do with anything?"

"That's what I'm trying to find out."

"Isn't that the job of the police?"

"They investigate their way, and I investigate mine." Cal paused. "Don't you want to know who's behind all of this?"

"I trust the police over some muckraking journalist."

"Look, Rebecca, I'm on your side."

"Are you?"

"Yes, I am. I'm just trying to figure out who has a motive for doing this to you."

"Probably Sid trying to torture me from the grave."

"Why would he want to torture you? Did he catch you having an affair?"

Rebecca glared at him. "Okay, you've gone too far this time. I'm done with you."

"So, he did catch you having an affair?"

She pointed to the door. "Out. Now!"

Cal gathered his things and shuffled toward the door.

"I did not have an affair. You can print that?"

He stopped and turned around, cocking his head to one side. "Are you sure you want me to print that? Or should I print these?" He held up his phone with the images that had been sent to him of a scantily-clad Rebecca engaged in what appeared to be some rather sensuous activity with a man who wasn't her husband.

"Where did you get those? Those are fake!"

"I'm sure they are. The truth, Rebecca?"

"Get out!"

Cal slipped out the back door and hopped the fence without looking back once. He'd obviously rattled the hive, and he had no doubt the queen bee would be after him soon.

***

EDDIE RAMSEY PULLED into the Seattle FC parking lot when his phone rang. It was his editor, Buckman.

"Boss, I don't have much time. What do you need?" he said as he answered.

"I swear, Ramsey, I'm gonna string you up when you get back to the office."

"Wha-what did I do?"

"I just got a call from Sid Westin's widow. I can't believe you'd threaten her like that."

"Whoa, whoa, whoa. Slow your roll, boss. I don't know what—"

"Save it. I can't believe you went to her house without talking to me first about it."

"But I—"

"I'm putting Cal back on the story. Get back to the office right now."

Ramsey ended the call and slammed his fist on the steering wheel. He seethed for a few minutes as he stared vacantly at the practice field in front of him.

Josh Moore tapped the window, snapping him out of his stupor. He motioned for Ramsey to roll down the window. Ramsey obliged.

"You gonna sit there all day or come inside and get to work?"

Ramsey sighed. "I swear if I see Cal Murphy again—"

"What'd Cal do to you this time?"

"I'm not sure, but it got me taken off this story."

Moore chuckled. "Well, he is a resourceful guy."

"You might find this funny, but I don't."

"Humor is always subjective."

"I'm gonna go give Cal a piece of my mind. Do you know where I might find him?"

Moore glanced at his watch. "It's almost noon, so you'll probably find him at King's Hardware off Ballard. It's his favorite lunchtime spot."

Ramsey didn't crack his door open, instead firing up the engine and zooming out of the parking lot.

***

CAL LEANED BACK as the bartender at King's slid a plate in front of him. The After School Special burger lay open faced while steam arose off the pile of fries. He oscillated between King's pulled pork sandwich and this giant mass of artery-blocking pub grub. Despite his intense love for barbecue, he once deviated at King's after one of the patrons offered to pay for his meal if he ordered the After School Special burger but didn't like it. Cal crinkled his nose at the thought of bacon and peanut butter on a burger—that is, until he tried it.

He placed the bun on top and mashed it down, forcing juice to drip down the sides. After taking hold of the monstrous burger, he glanced at it once more and smiled before raising it toward his mouth.

But the burger never made it there.

Cal jolted forward and nearly dropped his food as he suffered a shove from behind. Carefully setting down the burger, he spun around in his seat in time to catch the brunt of a right cross to his chin. He fell off his seat and staggered toward the ground. He put his hand down and caught himself in time to look up and see another punch headed his way.

Cal jumped upright and stepped back. He put both his hands out in an attempt to calm down his assailant.

"Eddie? What's gotten into you? I'm sure this is all just a big misunderstanding," he said as he stared at his seething colleague.

"Misunderstanding? Is that what you call impersonating me?"

"Hey, now. I don't know what you're talking about."

"Cut the bullshit, Cal. I figured out what you did. You weren't man enough to stand up to Buckman, so you sabotaged me to get back on the story."

"I'm afraid you've got it all wrong."

Ramsey lunged at Cal and acted as if he was going to take a swing at him before deciding otherwise. "Do I, Cal? Please tell me what I've got wrong."

"I wasn't trying to sabotage you, Ramsey. I just knew she would've never talked to me if I would've told her who I really was."

"I hope it was worth it."

Cal shrugged. "Perhaps. Time will tell."

Ramsey's eyes narrowed. "I oughta—"

"Oughta what, Ramsey? Admit to Buckman that you were the one who trashed him online last month on TheSportsReporters.com website? Tell him that it was you who called him a 'misogynistic drunk?'"

Mouth agape, Ramsey stared at Cal.

"What? You don't think the entire staff knows who the 'Emerald City King' is?"

"This is low, Cal—even for you."

"I never intended to get you in trouble."

"So what are you gonna do about it now?"

"I'm gonna get to the bottom of this—and apologize to Buckman later."

"How about just tell Buckman the truth now?"

Cal sighed. "I will, if you will—a joint meeting with Buckman. I'll tell him that I impersonated you, if you tell him that it was you who trashed him online. I know that's one mystery he's been dying to solve."

Ramsey's shoulders slumped as he looked downward. "Forget it. But you better watch yourself."

Cal nodded and slipped back onto his seat at the bar. "Let me buy you lunch, Ramsey. And I promise to clear this all up after I finish covering this story."

Ramsey sat down next to him. "Forget lunch. I'll just take a drink."

Cal motioned for the bartender to come over and asked him to put Ramsey's drinks on his bill.

"So what'd you learn from Sid Westin's widow?" Ramsey asked after he started nursing his scotch on the rocks.

"I don't know what she was up to, but she definitely wasn't an angel."

"Sounds like someone else I know."

"Sounds like everyone I know."

Ramsey took another long pull on his glass. "Are you always this cynical?"

"I'm not cynical—just real. People rarely surprise me any more. And least of all, grieving widows who were just served divorce papers."

Ramsey put down his drink hard on the bar. "Seriously?"

"Yeah. And that's not all. Whatever she was into, it

wasn't any good. And I suspect Sid found out about it."

"You think he threatened to rat her out and she had him killed?"

"It wouldn't surprise me, but there are more yarns in this story to pull on first."

CHAPTER 19

KITTRELL WHISTLED AS HE ENTERED the precinct. He felt fresh and strode into the office with a sense of purpose. After enduring weeks of ridicule—both in the press and in the office—he was ready to put it in the past by catching the gang that robbed the Puget Sound Bank. No longer would he and Quinn watch a room fall silent when they walked into it and suffer disappointing looks. They were going to be respected again and retain their position as the city's best detective duo.

"My, aren't we chipper this morning?" mumbled Charlotte Lawton as Kittrell walked by the reception desk. Lawton didn't look up as she pecked away on her keyboard. Standing as the first wave of defense against any person walking into the precinct, she had developed an uncanny ability to identify every personnel in the department—sometimes without even a glance—and deliver a snarky comment on demand. Behind her back, she was simply known as "The Watchman."

"It's Friday, Charlotte. Shouldn't we all be chipper?"

"Not if your suspect hung himself in custody last night," she muttered as she continued to type.

"Wha-what on earth are you talking about?" Kittrell said

as he dashed over to her desk. He leaned forward, trying to draw her full attention. "Please tell me that you're playing a cruel joke on me."

She finally took her fingers off the keyboard and looked up at him. "I wish I were, honey."

He glanced behind her toward the endless rows of desks and cubicles. He locked eyes with Quinn from across the room. Quinn saw him and shook his head.

Kittrell let out a string of expletives as he stormed back toward Quinn.

"What happened last night?" Kittrell demanded.

Quinn broke into a coughing fit before he spoke. "Apparently, our good buddy Wayne Geller hung himself in his cell with his bed sheet." He handed Kittrell a report.

Kittrell opened the report and started to peruse it. "Why wasn't he placed on suicide watch?"

"Did you think he was a threat to kill himself after speaking with him yesterday?"

Kittrell shook his head.

"Neither did I."

"Has anyone told Chief yet?"

Quinn forced a smile. "I thought I'd save that honor for you." He started coughing again.

"Aren't you a gem?" Kittrell snarled. Then he paused. "You okay?"

Quinn pounded his chest a couple of times. "I'm fine. Just the start of something."

"Pneumonia?"

"Let's hope not."

In silence, the two detectives walked down the hall toward Chief Roman's office. Kittrell tried to rehearse in his head the best way to break the news to the chief. He debated for a moment before deciding on a direct delivery.

Kittrell knocked lightly on the door that was slightly cracked.

"Come in," Roman said.

Kittrell gently pushed it open.

Roman wore a wide grin on his face and took a sip of his coffee. He set it down on his desk and looked at the two detectives. "What happened to you two? You both look like your dog just died."

"Close enough. Our suspect, Wayne Geller, hung himself in his cell last night," Kittrell said as he tossed the file folder on Roman's desk.

"How come this is the first I'm hearing of this?" he said as he started to flip through the report.

"Probably because nobody wanted to ruin your Friday," Quinn quipped.

"It's sufficiently ruined now," Roman growled. "So what are we gonna do about this mess now? Our one link to the robbery is now dead."

Kittrell shrugged. "I guess we'll circle back with forensics and see if they've got anything else that could help us identify some of the other members of this crew."

Roman slammed his fists down on the desk and started cursing. "And just after I assured the city council members that we had this all under control. Why is this world always trying to screw me over?" He looked up at the detectives. "Are we sure Geller wasn't helped, if you know what I mean?"

"We'll look at the report and talk to the officers who discovered him and let you know what we find."

"Check the surveillance footage," Roman said. "This just seems strange to me."

"Us too, Chief," Quinn said.

Kittrell put his knuckles down on Roman's desk and leaned forward. "Don't worry, Chief. This isn't going to turn into another Arnold Grayson situation. We'll find these guys."

Roman took another sip of his coffee. "You better. My patience is running thin."

CHAPTER 20

CAL LOOKED AT HIS PHONE and saw Kelly's name pop up on the screen. He'd have to be honest with her about what had happened—and he braced for her reaction.

"You did what?!" she said. "Have you lost your mind?"

"Buckman pulled me off the case. What was I supposed to do?" he protested.

"Figure out another way—a way that didn't involve sabotaging another reporter's livelihood."

"I'll tell Buckman as soon as I'm done covering the story."

"And how'd you get Ramsey to go along with that?"

"Maybe I have something on him."

"Cal! Come on now. You're better than this. You need to fight your battles the right way."

"I know something's going on here, Kelly. And I know that Ramsey would never figure it out. He's lazy."

"What about the Seattle PD?"

"I don't have much confidence that they'll figure this out, either. Look, I know it seems like I'm crossing the line with some of the things I'm doing, but it's all to find out why Sid Westin was murdered."

"And what if he wasn't? What if it was all just part of a robbery gone bad? What then?"

Cal sighed. "If it was only that easy. When you know, you know."

"I'm disappointed in you, Cal. I thought you were better than this."

"If I'm bending the rules, it's only so the person who took Westin's life suffers just consequences."

"But confronting his widow and pretending to be someone else?"

"Okay, look, I'm sure I could've gone about it another way. But as each day goes by and his killers walk free, it makes it that much more difficult to track him down. I can't let that happen."

"You just better be glad I'm not there to straighten you out."

"You're doing just fine from where you are."

"About that, Cal. I don't know if you've been paying attention to the national news lately, but there's a huge late winter storm sweeping through the Southeast this week, and I doubt we'll be able to make it back by Sunday."

"Really? A big late winter snowstorm is going to hit the Southeast? I think the last one predicted to hit there when we lived back east generated a whopping half inch of snow."

"They're projecting eight to ten inches for Saturday night," she said. "And as you know, that's going to cripple this entire state, not to mention city and airport."

"So, how much longer do you think you'll be there?"

"I don't know—a few more days. Not that Maddie minds. She's being spoiled rotten by my mother."

"Okay. Stay warm and keep me updated."

"I will—and you better cut out the shenanigans, Cal. I'll be home soon enough."

Cal hung up and opened his laptop. While he had been

pulled off the Sid Westin story and banished from the Seattle FC practice grounds for the time being, he still had one more story to write on the team—and it was due tomorrow.

Buckman still wanted the piece on Seattle's new young star, Shawn Lynch. And Cal was going to give it to him.

He spent the rest of his morning pounding out the feature story on Lynch, but he felt it was missing something. There were a few quotes from Lynch, but most of them were from other people, including his father. Cal needed one or two more solid comments to solidify his lead paragraph.

I know just the guy.

He dialed Javier Martinez's number and prayed he would answer so he could spend the rest of his day doing something he'd been warned by both his editor and wife against doing.

I could have a worse vice and drink myself into oblivion like most of my colleagues.

Cal knew it was a lame excuse in an attempt to justify his rogue behavior, but he'd been covering these types of stories long enough to learn that everyone justifies what they do, for better or worse. Over the years, he'd learned from the masters at how to fabricate a reasonably sounding justification. If forced to look at it objectively, he knew it was full of more holes than the Cleveland Browns defensive front. But at least for the moment, nobody outside of his wife or Ramsey knew what he was doing. And neither of them would be questioning him about his methods for a few days at least.

Martinez's phone rang a few times, but he didn't pick up. After the sixth ring, his voicemail came on.

"I'm out playing the beautiful game or enjoying this beautiful world. You know what to do." Beep.

Cal hung up. He'd try again later.

He pushed back from the desk in his home office and propped his feet up. He put his hands behind his head and stared out the window at the cedar waxwing birds hopping on a tree branch in his backyard. Cedar waxwings were incredibly social birds and appeared to enjoy grooming one another. Cal watched with delight as the two birds traded duties of picking loose objects like dirt and twigs off one another with their beaks. They didn't just survive but thrived because they worked together.

It's a lost art among humans. At least some species on earth understands the concept of cooperation.

The sound of his phone buzzing on his desk jolted him out of his philosophical trance.

He glanced at his phone but didn't recognize the number. It was a text message with an attachment icon in the upper corner.

What's this? More spam?

He opened the email attachment that began with a brief message.

> Guess when this photo was taken? While Sid
> Westin was playing his final away game.

Cal pulled his phone closer to his face and struggled to see the significance of the photo. It was a picture of Rebecca Westin standing in front of a sports car, making a sultry pose, including the puckered lips that Cal detested so much. He told Kelly more times than he could count that if he ever saw her puckering out her lips like a demented duck that he'd take her phone away. It was all in good fun as he knew she was in lockstep with him over their disdain for such ridiculous poses. "This is why the aliens will never land here," Kelly once told him. And he wholeheartedly agreed.

He stared at the picture of Rebecca for a few more moments but didn't see anything that would warrant a mysterious text. Cal loathed Instagram and other forms of social media, even if he had to join the various social networks per Buckman's order, though he was certain this picture must've appeared on one of the social network sites. But despite his best efforts, he couldn't make out anything scandalous. He decided to write the mystery texter back.

Who is this?

He waited a moment until he received a response.

Look more closely in the window of the car

Before Cal could blow the picture up, the image vanished from his screen as Javier Martinez's name and face popped up for an incoming call.

Nice timing, Martinez.

Cal answered the call. "Javy! How are you?"

"Did you call me, Cal?"

"I need a couple more comments from Seattle FC's quote machine."

Martinez laughed. "I do what I can. What do you need, brother?"

"I'm finishing up my story on Lynch, and I wanted to get a couple of comments from you regarding his maturation as a player. What has he done, in your opinion, to grow up so fast?"

"On the record or off the record?"

"Is there something about Lynch I should know?"

"For your story—and on the record—Lynch is one of the most dedicated players we've got. He arrives earlier and stays later than any other player on the team. He's always trying to improve personally, and it's paid big dividends for our team."

"This is great. Just a sec." Cal typed furiously as he transcribed Martinez's comments in real time. It helped that he talked more slowly than some of his other Latino brethren. "Okay," Cal said as he finished. "What about this off the record stuff?"

"Well, this is all hearsay, so I can't verify any of this," Martinez began, "but I've heard a few whispers around the clubhouse from guys who think he's using."

"Performance enhancers?"

"Yeah. And it doesn't surprise me either."

"What do you mean?"

"It's not uncommon for a young player to add weight and strength once they arrive in the league and get the proper training. Dumbbells, diets, and drills—the 'triple D effect', as it's commonly referred to in our locker room. Awful name, I know, but no crude jokes, please."

"No jokes, I promise," Cal said with a smirk. "Go on."

"Usually, the triple D effect makes a moderate impact on a player. They all get stronger, sharper and swifter—"

"The Triple S results?" Cal quipped.

"Look, I don't make up these lame names. I'm just telling you the story, okay?"

"Got it. Please continue."

"Well, our trainer who's been around the league since it started back more than twenty years ago said that Lynch's results are off the chart. He's never had anybody within twenty percent of what he's accomplished in the time he's been here. And he emphasized legally."

"Meaning guys have equaled or surpassed what he's done illegally?"

"That's what I inferred from his comments."

"So, is Lynch using?"

"The whispers around the clubhouse are that it's only a matter of time before he gets caught. Players would love to turn his cocky self in, but we're all benefitting from his improved play. And quite frankly we need all the help we can get right now after Sid's passing."

"You really think he's going to get suspended?"

"Not think—know. You can't get away with that in this day and age. If he's raising the eyebrows of our trainer, I know plenty of other people around the league are looking suspiciously at Lynch."

"Thanks, Martinez. You've been a valuable help to my story—for both this one and some future ones I'm likely to write."

"Just keep my name out of those future ones, Cal."

"You know I will."

Cal hung up and took a deep breath. He wanted to contemplate for a moment if he should even write the story given what Martinez told him. Or perhaps he could simply tell Buckman and let him decide. Either way, it was a mess. But Cal didn't have long to dwell on that potential bomb before he remembered the photo of Rebecca Westin.

Rebecca's voluptuous figure filled his screen. He zoomed in on the picture, trying to see what the anonymous person was trying to get him to see. It took him a few minutes. But after twisting his phone and scanning the picture, finally he saw it. And he wasted no time in asking again who the mysterious texter was:

Who is this?

Nothing. He waited for a few more minutes before concluding that he wasn't going to hear from anybody. With all the scandals he was uncovering, Cal thought about checking his calendar to see if today was indeed Christmas. It certainly felt like it to him.

His phone rang again with another number he didn't recognize.

"This is Cal Murphy."

"Cal, this is detective Mel Kittrell from the Seattle PD. We need to talk."

CHAPTER 21

MEL KITTRELL WAVED the waitress over to his table and pointed at his coffee cup. She obliged his unspoken request and filled it up sufficiently, leaving just enough room for him to add cream or sugar. He scowled and motioned for her to continue pouring.

"Real men don't add anything to their coffee," he grumbled as she stopped filling up his mug just a hair's width before it overflowed. "It puts hair on your chest."

The waitress forced a smile before she scurried away to another table demanding her presence.

The bell on the door jangled against the glass, drawing Kittrell's attention along with the other four patrons in the restaurant. It was Cal Murphy, who kept his head down except to glance around the room and identify who he was scheduled to meet. Kittrell watched as Cal walked nonchalantly toward him before sliding into the booth seat opposite of him.

"Thanks for coming," Kittrell said.

Cal shrugged. "Not sure I can be of much help, but I'll try. Where's your partner?"

"He's got a nasty case of the flu. I prefer not to see him again for at least another week."

"I don't blame you."

The waitress bounced back toward their table and turned over the plain white mug sitting in front of Cal.

"Coffee?" she said, unwilling to wait for Cal's response. She filled his cup halfway before he had a chance to respond.

"Thanks," he said as he stared down at the steaming liquid in front of him. "So, what's this all about?" Cal began as he redirected his attention toward Kittrell. "And before we begin, full disclosure—I'm back on this story."

Kittrell furrowed his brow. "When were you ever off it?"

"A couple of days ago, but I fixed that."

"What happened?"

"Someone with vested interest in this story put pressure on my boss to get me off the story, but I pulled a few strings to rectify the matter."

"Legally?"

Cal scrunched up his face and shrugged as his head bobbed from side to side.

"Never mind. You don't have to answer that. In fact, I don't wanna know."

"Fair enough. So, what's this all about?"

"I think we both know by now that Sid Westin wasn't just an innocent bystander killed during an armed robbery."

"I'm beginning to have my doubts about the innocent bystander thing."

"You're just beginning to have doubts?"

"Look, Detective. I can't imagine it'd be much different in your world than mine. I can't print anything until I've got some verifiable proof—the kind of proof that we can leverage to escape a messy lawsuit if one happens to appear. And right now, as much as my gut is telling me that something is awry here, I don't have the kind of proof required."

Kittrell slapped the table and grinned. "Well, you're wrong. My world is very different—at least at this point it is. I'm simply tasked with coming up with a theory. Nothing has to be confirmed or verified yet. That all comes later. I just need to develop a plausible theory and work it until its logical conclusion."

"And what theory are you working right now?"

"The one that says Rebecca Westin is behind all of this."

Cal eyed him cautiously. "What makes you say that?"

"Evidence, to be honest. Though if I was backed into a corner, I'd say most of it was circumstantial. But Rebecca will benefit the most from Sid's death."

"That's far from news. Aren't most spouses the primary beneficiary of their spouse?"

"Unless there's a written will, yes. But in the case of a young husband dying, that's almost always an easy out."

"Why is it not only easy but also correct this time around?"

"For one, we've already been able to tie the vehicle the bank robbers used back to the Westins."

Cal smiled and held up his hand. "Is this on the record or off? I just want to clarify."

"For now, it's off. But help me solve this thing and that will all change."

"I'm listening."

"The unfortunate part of my story is that our chief witness in the story hung himself in his jail cell after he agreed to cooperate."

"Sounds fishy to me?"

Kittrell's eyes widened as he stared at Cal for a moment before speaking, "That's what I said. Nobody at the department was listening to me." He sighed. "And to be honest, I never imagined he would take his own life."

"That's because he didn't."

Kittrell nodded at Cal. "You've got a point—a point that fell on deaf ears when I made it at the department right after it happened."

"But right now, there are just too many things aligning for Rebecca not to be the killer." Cal leaned back in his seat. "Way too many."

"Is there something I should know about?" Kittrell asked.

Cal fished his cell phone out of his pocket and tapped in the security code. He navigated to the correct page and slid the phone across the table to the sergeant. "Take a look at this."

Kittrell cocked his head to one side as he took the phone and stared at the page on the screen. He squinted as he stared at the image. "What am I looking at here?"

"This picture was supposedly taken and posted when Sid Westin was out of town for Seattle FC's last road game."

"I get that, but what am I looking at?"

Cal took another sip of his coffee. "I think the better question is who, Detective."

"How'd you get this photo?" Kittrell said, his gaze darting from the screen to Cal.

"Someone sent it to me."

"Did they obtain it legally?"

"Doubt it. Look in the window in the background."

Kittrell zoomed on the picture and gawked at the image on the screen.

"Do you see it?" Cal asked.

Kittrell chuckled to himself. "Oh, I see it all right. I just want to know who that is."

"Look a little closer."

After a few seconds, Kittrell smacked his forehead with his hand. "Is that who I think it is?"

Cal nodded. "Yep. Sid Westin's agent, Jonathan Umbert."

"What was he doing with Rebecca Westin?"

"Your guess is as good as mine, but I can almost guarantee you they weren't going over Sid's latest contract."

Kittrell shook his head. "This just got really interesting."

CHAPTER 22

CAL FILED HIS STORY on Lynch and took a call from Buckman less than fifteen minutes later. According to Buckman, he'd received an email from an anonymous source with footage of Cal's confrontation with Ramsey at King's Hardware. Buckman went into a tirade, complete with yelling, cursing, and threatening. Buckman's bluster didn't bother Cal too much as he'd experience a far more emotional Buckman when the curmudgeon once exploded in a staff meeting over the inability to apply the Oxford comma in various articles in that day's edition.

"Finally," Buckman said, "I'm taking you off this story completely. You are done, Cal. I can't believe you acted like this toward a fellow colleague. You're lucky I didn't fire you over this."

Cal knew better than to concoct some excuse. Enduring a tongue lashing from his wife was sufficient. Buckman was only telling Cal what he already knew.

He hung up and let out a guttural growl. Knowing Ramsey the way he did, Cal suspected this was his doing. It was confirmed less than five minutes later when Cal received a text message from Ramsey with nothing but an emoji sticking its tongue out.

I wish that was your face so I could punch it right now, you spineless punk.

It was too late to dwell on what he should have done to get himself back on the story. Violence wasn't the answer—and he knew it. All his justifications felt lame and contrived and desperate. He was driven by both the desire to atone for missing on the Gonzalez story as well as his dogged determination to get the truth out. But Kelly was right that he knew better, and it was nothing more than an impulsive decision to try and reassert himself in one of the most important stories in the city to come along in the past few years, even if it didn't seem that way to anyone else.

A bank robbery that resulted in the death of one of the city's most beloved sports stars was a shame, yet that story that didn't have many legs. But a murder disguised as a bank robbery? The latter was the kind of story sadistic reporters dream about. And Cal fell squarely into that category. He craved stories with angles galore and legs that would carry them for miles of column space on the front page. While he felt like his ability to worm his way back into Buckman's good graces might appear like an insurmountable challenge, he knew he'd find a way back armed with the truth of what really happened—as long as he beat Ramsey to it.

The questions of who and why gnawed at Cal as he mulled over his hypothesis that the bank robbery was all a cover for the blatant murder of Sid Westin. Rebecca, Sid's wife, was looking more and more guilty by the moment—and perhaps she was aided by Umbert. Or maybe Umbert planned the whole thing so he could have Rebecca all to himself. At this point, Cal couldn't be sure, but he wasn't going to rule anything out either. And there was still the possibility that none of these scenarios were correct.

He slammed his laptop shut and headed out the door, destined for the downtown Seattle PD precinct to meet up with Kittrell.

***

WHEN CAL ENTERED the precinct, he was met by a few familiar faces—some friendly and some not so much. Cal saw the chief and nodded at him. The chief nodded back and then glanced at his coffee cup that appeared as if it had been ejected from a machine in the break room. Cal watched the chief take a sip and then glance back over in his direction.

Cal began to grow nervous, even though he had no reason to be concerned. His nerves returned when he saw Kittrell walk up to the chief, slap him on the back with a case folder, and share a laugh together.

"You ready to do this?" Kittrell asked as he neared Cal.

Cal nodded. "Ready as I'll ever be."

The two agreed to work together on questioning Umbert. Since Cal wasn't on the case any longer, Kittrell told him he'd ask the chief about letting him join as a special consultant. With Cal's knowledge of all the principle suspects involved, Kittrell believed it would benefit the department to have him join in. At least that's what Cal heard. He wondered if this whole show of partnership was nothing more than to keep an eye on *The Times'* feisty reporter who often stirred up trouble for the Seattle PD. Cal decided he'd honor his word not to write about the case as long as he was working on it with Kittrell. But Cal knew the minute the heart of the story broke, he'd resign as a consultant. There was no way he was going to give this story to anyone else in the department—especially Ramsey.

They took Kittrell's car, and the two engaged in small talk as the detective navigated Seattle's late afternoon traffic with relative ease.

"How do you know about all these shortcuts?" Cal asked, half awed, half jealous over Kittrell's prowess on the streets.

"GPS directions are so overrated. They send everyone down the same beaten path. Meanwhile, if you have a good sense of direction and a good idea about traffic flow patterns, it's not difficult to maneuver around the so-called preferred routes with ease."

"So, have you developed any alternate theories about Umbert yet?" Cal asked.

"I haven't had time to." Kittrell glanced over at Cal. "But at this point, do we really need to? It seems pretty open and shut to me—as long as we can gather the evidence to prove Umbert had something to do with it."

"That might not be so easy."

"Well, you might be right."

Cal eyed the detective cautiously. "What are you not telling me?"

He sighed. "The getaway van used by the robbers was in Sid Westin's name."

"Come again?"

"I think you heard me loud and clear."

"Yeah, but I don't believe it. How is that even possible?"

"Rebecca claims she didn't even know her husband owned a van."

"But you've verified that he did?"

Kittrell nodded. "Apparently it was a big secret. There were a few other people who knew about it. We tracked down the guy Sid bought the van from just to make sure it was indeed Sid—and the seller confirmed it was."

"So you think Rebecca found out about the van and used it to frame him?"

"Maybe. I think we need to catch Umbert off guard first and get a bead on him before we start firming up theories."

A few minutes later, they pulled into the parking garage where Umbert's office was located. The sign for Umbert & Associates was both bold and elegant, the signature name highlighting the top of the twelve-story office building and sending the message Umbert obviously intended to send with his business: rich and powerful.

"I don't understand why these sports agents spend so much money on their office space," Kittrell wondered aloud. "They're just negotiating contracts for professional athletes; it's not like they need all this."

"Would you want to hire an agent who worked out of his garage?" Cal asked as they entered the lobby.

"Great things have come out of garages over the years."

"But they don't stay there."

They stepped onto the elevator and began ascending to the top floor.

Kittrell shrugged. "To each his own, I guess. If I was collecting ten percent of these players' monster contracts, I'd still work out of my garage. It'd be a posh garage, mind you. But I wouldn't leave the house."

"Maybe it's a good thing you're not an agent then."

The elevator came to a halt and the doors slid open, revealing the ritzy office environment of Umbert's business. Plush leather couches and chairs, Italian marbled floors, multiple flat screen HD televisions inset into oak wood panels, a small fountain covered with coins on the bottom—not pennies, but golden one dollar coins.

The duo took in the scene for a moment before locating

the front desk and heading toward it.

"You think your garage would look like this?" Cal whispered.

Kittrell shook his head. "Nope. Never like this—even if I was an agent."

Cal smiled as he approached the svelte young woman with blonde hair who returned his smile before speaking.

"What can I help you gentlemen with today?" she asked.

"I'm Detective Kittrell, and this is my special consultant, Cal Murphy. We were hoping to speak with Mr. Umbert today about an ongoing investigation."

Her face fell. "I'm sorry, but Mr. Umbert isn't in the office right now."

"Do you know when he'll be back? We can wait."

"You'll be waiting a while. He's in London this week on business."

"What's he doing in London?" Cal said.

She tilted her head to one side. "Apparently another young soccer player wants to play for Seattle FC, and he's going to meet with him. It was all very last minute."

"Do you know when he's scheduled to return?" Kittrell asked.

"I'm not sure. He asked me to purchase him an open-ended ticket. I can let him know that you stopped by when he calls to check in, if you like."

Kittrell held up his hand. "That won't be necessary. Thanks for your time."

They turned away from the desk and headed toward the elevator. Once inside, they waited until the doors closed until either of them spoke.

"He leaves the country now," Kittrell said. "How convenient."

"No way this was a coincidence."

CHAPTER 23

THE NEXT MORNING, Cal took advantage of his girls being out of town and decided to get in a morning run at the Queen Anne Greenbelt before feasting at his favorite breakfast haunt, The 5 Spot. Although he didn't have as much time to run as he used to, his decision to run for nearly an hour on the greenbelt had more to do with guilt for what he was about to eat rather than for what he'd already eaten. With Kelly out of town, Cal's diet was reduced to little more than fast food and greasy spoons. He'd made significant changes to his dietary habits since he married Kelly, but he hated to miss an opportunity to indulge in some of his guilty pleasures from yesteryear. In his mind, the long run mitigated the ill-effects of The 5 Spot's biscuits and gravy dish he was craving before he sat down and opened up a copy of *The Times*.

Cal decided to re-read his article on Shawn Lynch to make sure some copy editor didn't exchange his tight prose for something deemed more nuanced and gripping. He'd never been married to every word he wrote in a story, but he hated it when his stories were unrecognizable after an editor decided to justify his or her existence. One of the reasons he enjoyed working for Buckman was his philosophy that editors were there to improve upon an existing piece of work—and nothing else. However, the ambiguous and subjective definition as to what qualified as "improved" often-times created angst between Cal and the copy desk.

Yet for the most part, Cal's article remained untouched save a few spots where the writing was tightened. His story highlighted Shawn Lynch's ascension through the ranks of the Seattle FC team and how he'd become a solid corner-stone for the team to move forward. He related a story about how Lynch sold his coach on his ability to create scoring op-portunities and how Lynch's salesmanship was only rivaled by his ability to score goals.

From there, Cal's story transitioned with this line: "But that shouldn't come as a surprise to anyone who's lived in Seattle longer than a week and heard his father's catchy jingle on the radio or television about his automobile conglomerate named Cars, Cars, Cars."

Cal figured he could count on one hand the number of times he'd been driving in Seattle and not been within an arm's length of at least two other automobiles that didn't have a Cars, Cars, Cars nameplate affixed to the trunk or the company logo emblazoned on the license plate tag holder. Seattle residents often joked that they bought their latest car from Cars, Cars, Cars just so he'd stop advertising. Yet lining William Lynch's pockets with more revenue resulted only in a more substantial marketing budget—which meant more commercials on local TV and radio stations.

However, Cal didn't mind. He found the senior Lynch's commercials plenty amusing, mostly due to the fact that the old man liked to ride horses in the commercials. The irony wasn't lost on Cal, who wondered if William Lynch was sim-ply a man who time had forgotten. There was little doubt in

Cal's mind that if the elder Lynch had been born a hundred years earlier than he was, he would've sold more horses to cowboys than anyone in the Pacific Northwest. Even as he put down the newspaper to take a sip of his coffee, he looked up on the television to see William Lynch galloping onto the screen while swinging a rope. The camera panned in awkwardly on Lynch's face as he expressed delight over what he'd done. When the camera pulled away, he was reeling in a zero percentage sign, which was the popular selling hook for the moment.

The two old men crammed into the table next to him were complaining loudly about everything from the weather to politics to new technology. They both stopped what they were talking about to gawk at the commercial before a new rant began.

"Hasn't that guy stolen enough people's money already?" groused one of the men, who was wearing a hound's tooth hat and tapping his cane to emphasize certain words.

"It's bad enough he's fleeced half of Seattle; the least he could do would be to spare us these commercials. These things are so bad, he makes the marketing team for LifeCall seem like advertising geniuses and…" The elderly gentleman started wheezing and coughing, and Cal couldn't make out the rest of the man's sentence.

The other man held up his newspaper and pointed to Cal's article. "And now we have to read about him and his son in *The Times*. I swear if I still had my license, I'd—"

"Excuse me," Cal said, temporarily halting their joint rant. "I couldn't help but overhear you two talking about William Lynch. What did you mean when you said he's 'stolen enough people's money?' Is there something I should know about Cars, Cars, Cars?"

The man with the hat looked Cal up and down. "Are you new in town?"

"I've been around a while, but perhaps maybe not as long as you two have. Just trying to glean some wisdom here."

The other man pointed at Cal. "Hey, I know you. Aren't you that sports writer for *The Times*? I think I've seen you in some ads or interviewed on television before."

Cal nodded. "Guilty as charged." He offered his hand to the men. "Cal Murphy from *The Times*."

The man in the hat shook Cal's hand. "Ed Mueller."

"Casper Thornbush."

The two old men both looked down at the newspaper on their table.

"And you wrote this article?" Mueller asked.

Cal nodded. "I'm afraid so."

"And you don't know the truth about William Lynch?"

Cal shrugged. "I only know what I know. If there's more to him than low-budget car commercials, I'd love to learn about it."

"William Lynch—or, more precisely, one of his minions—runs an underground sports book in the city," Mueller said. "It's one of Seattle's worst-kept secrets. I can't believe you haven't heard of it if you've lived here longer than a month or two."

Cal took another sip of his coffee before responding. "I've tried to expose organized crime rings in the past, and I've found it to be very dangerous to my health, not to mention my family's."

Thornbush's eyes widened beneath his thick glasses, creating an optical effect that forced Cal to suppress a smile. "You better stay away from Lynch then. He has his tentacles in every aspect of this city."

Mueller shifted in his seat. "That's why I knew your story about the baseball player—what's his name?"

"Gonzalez," Cal answered.

"Yes, Gonzalez. I knew that story was a crock the moment I read it. Nailing Gonzalez was a big win for the FBI, even if someone in the department told you they wanted a bigger fish. That was a pipe dream. No way they were going to catch Lynch. He's too good to get caught."

"And even if he were to get caught, his goons would have leverage on someone to make sure the evidence was suppressed. There's no doubt in my mind that's what happened with Gonzalez."

Thornbush nodded in agreement.

"How come I've never heard about any of this?" Cal said.

"We both worked at the docks for years. It's a great place to hunt for guys looking for some supplemental income who have special skills," Thornbush said. "Maybe it's not as common knowledge as we think, but it's not a state secret, I can tell ya that much."

Cal faked a frightened look and lied. "Well, I'll do my best to steer clear." The truth was all he needed was a sports angle and he was all in.

What are sports without betting?

His fresh dream of mounting a surprise attack on William Lynch and crashing his empire ended quickly when Mueller delivered some ominous words.

"It's too late for that, I'm afraid."

Cal looked quizzically at Mueller. "What do you mean?"

"I can almost guarantee you that one of his men will pay you a visit after that article you just wrote."

"What are you talking about?"

"You dared to mention that his son suddenly bulked up last season which baffled his teammates. Savvy readers know what you were insinuating."

"And you think William Lynch will have someone come pay me a visit because of that one line in the article?"

"I'd bet the farm on it. Either way, you're on his radar now, so you best be careful."

Cal fished a twenty-dollar bill out of his wallet and placed it on the table. He stood up and looked at the two men. "I appreciate this candid conversation, gentlemen. Hopefully, you won't hear from me in *The Times*' obituary section. But if you do, at least you'll have an idea about what happened to me."

Cal slid his chair under his table and exited the restaurant. He began walking back toward the greenbelt where he'd parked, these new revelations weighing heavily upon him. The news that Gonzalez's indictment actually wasn't the focus of the FBI's pursuit of an illegal gambling ring ignited Cal's ire. The senior Lynch's finagling and meddling in the investigation resulted in making him look like a misinformed reporter at best, a sloppy one at worst. And Cal took this personally, even though he was sane enough to admit that this wasn't a conspiracy against him.

Before he began mulling over a way to bring Lynch's illegal empire to its knees—and save Seattle from any more of the worst low-budget commercials ever aired—he was shoved into an alley and sent sprawling to the ground.

Cal tried to stand up but didn't make it before a boot connected with his ribs. He crashed back down to the ground, splashing into a small pool of standing water. Moaning, he started to stand up again before he was yanked to his feet and held against the wall.

Cal looked toward the alleyway entrance in hopes that someone might see them, but his view was impeded by a dumpster. He was left to face his attacker.

"What do you want?" Cal asked.

The man who'd hit him was wearing a mask, revealing nothing more than average brown eyes and a slightly crooked mouth.

"Mr. Lynch didn't appreciate what you wrote in today's paper about his son," the man said. "He wants you to write another article about him that explains how he bulked up. Such insinuations could be detrimental to his career. And Mr. Lynch will hold you responsible if anything negative results from what you wrote."

Cal sighed and winced as he pressed on his aching rib cage. "Unfortunately, I'm not permitted to write about Seattle FC anymore. You'll need to get someone else to do Mr. Lynch's bidding."

"No, you need to clean up this mess. Otherwise, it will be unfortunate for you." The man poked Cal in the chest, emphasizing the word you before he sucker-punched him again in the gut.

Cal staggered to the ground and looked up in time to see the man sprinting in the opposite direction.

The old men weren't joking about William Lynch's powerful influence over the city.

Cal had just poked a bear he didn't even know existed.

CHAPTER 24

KITTRELL'S SATURDAY MORNING BEGAN by shuffling along the sidewalk of 5th Street until he reached Columbia and took a right. Outside of Seattle, grabbing a morning cup of coffee at Starbucks would've been considered a traitorous act, a brazen show of support for an established corporation. But inside Seattle, it was considered shopping local. Not to mention that Kittrell needed the strong, bold flavor that only Starbucks offered. If he could've bypassed it all for a shot of adrenaline, he would have.

Chief Roman scuttled Kittrell's Friday evening plans when he leaned on him to produce some results. Quinn threatened to crawl out of bed and assist Kittrell by reviewing the files, but Kittrell insisted his partner remain at home resting. Catching Quinn's nasty bug would slow down Kittrell, and that was something the chief explained wouldn't be tolerated.

Their brief successful capture of Wayne Geller left Chief Roman craving a win—a big win. He wanted to solve the case on the robbery that left Sid Westin dead and gain some closure for all parties involved. Everyone on the force united around this desire, but it wasn't translating into finding another person involved in the robbery. Or even solid leads for that matter.

Kittrell had spent a good portion of his Friday night combing through surveillance footage in the surrounding area and digging through Geller's phone records to uncover a connection to the other robbers. But he'd come up empty. All the numbers Geller called from the phone he had with him were to burner phones. It was nearly impossible to link them to another person—and Kittrell was finding this to be true.

Once he reached his desk and began sucking down his Starbucks, Kittrell tried to think of any ways to identify and locate any of Geller's accomplices. Old girlfriends, former employers, relatives, bar haunts—they'd all resulted in nothing significant. His ideas were drying up fast.

A knock on the side of his cubicle brought him out of his personal doldrums.

"Detective, I've got something you might be interested in," said Woody Franks, a fellow detective, as he tossed an envelope with the name Phil's Paint Shop scrawled on the front onto Kittrell's desk. "Some guy dropped this off at the front desk. Said you'd requested the footage from his surveillance camera and he was out of town until last night."

Kittrell picked up the envelope and dumped out the flash drive. "Did he say what was on it?"

Franks shrugged. "I'm just relaying a message, but not that I know of. He didn't know what we were looking for, did he?"

"Thanks, Franks. I'll take a look at it."

"Chin up, Kittrell. Roman's feeling the heat right now, but he's a realist. He won't hold it against you forever."

Kittrell looked down at his desk. "That's not helping."

"Better you than me." Franks winked. "Later." He disappeared around a corridor.

Kittrell sat still for a moment and then got up and wandered down the hall in search of someone on the forensics team to help him dissect the evidence. He couldn't even remember where this business was, but he figured it must've been important if he put in a request for security camera footage. After fifteen minutes of wandering the halls looking for help, he gave up and found a studio to examine what was on the drive himself.

"I've seen them do this a thousand times," Kittrell muttered aloud. "I'm sure I can figure this out."

In less than five minutes, the computer started to whirr. Kittrell jammed the flash drive into an open USB port and started clicking. He found the digital time stamp that aligned with the time the robbery occurred. The images jutted by on the screen for several minutes, yet nothing appeared to be significant. At least, not yet anyway.

Then a flash on the screen—and Kittrell froze. He backed up the footage and slowed it down to make sure what he saw was actually happening. He paused on a frame showing a white van pulling into a discreet garage entrance in a back alleyway behind the business. Zooming in on the license plate, he wrote it down on a sticky note and rushed back to his desk to check his files. He dug out some of his files and located the report about Sid Westin's white van. The license plate numbers matched.

He'd done this a thousand times, but his heart always started racing when he collected a piece of evidence that could help him catch a perp. Rushing back to the studio, he opened a web browser and searched for the address of Phil's Paint Shop. He needed to determine the approximate location affiliated with the garage entrance.

"Gotcha!" Kittrell yelled. He scratched down the street

name and number on a sticky note again and sprinted back to his desk. He re-read the address back to himself: 860 Harrison Street.

He started to dial Chief Roman's number to tell him that they needed to get a SWAT team over there—or at least a forensics team to comb the place. But as Cal was dialing the number, he heard dispatch squawk something on the scanner that made him freeze.

We've got a possible 187 reported at 860 Harrison Street. Requesting assistance.

Kittrell glanced down at his note. The addresses matched.

He didn't waste any time. He grabbed his keys and jacket before sprinting out the door to his car. As a frequent patron of nearby favorite pizza joint, Serious Pie & Biscuit, he knew the area well. It wasn't any more than a ten-minute drive even in rush hour traffic.

As he drove, Kittrell hoped against hope that it was a mistake, that perhaps he got it wrong and the address was 840 or 850. He'd been wrong before, but not often—yet he'd never wanted to be so wrong in his life.

When his car skidded to a stop in the alleyway behind the store, he didn't bother to shut the door as he got out and ran toward the flashing lights. Two cars had beat him to the scene, and all the officers had their guns drawn.

"Come check this out," one of the officers shouted.

Kittrell rushed inside the garage and flashed his badge at one of the other officers. He scanned the area and couldn't believe what he saw. Three bodies were scattered throughout what appeared to be a staging area for the robbers.

He couldn't be sure what happened, but he tried to cobble together a theory. Given that the men lying dead around the room were indeed scumbags, Kittrell didn't feel much remorse or sadness over their deaths. One of these men had killed another innocent unarmed man in cold blood. And for what? For fun? Because he could?

No matter what the reason, Kittrell couldn't say he was displeased over the end result. He stepped over one of the bodies as if it were a stump on a trail in the woods.

"Greedy bastards," one of the officers said aloud as he looked down at an alleged thief still grasping a stack of hundred dollar bills. "Probably killed each other over money."

One of the officers looked up and saw Kittrell. He'd worked with Kittrell before on several cases, and it was common knowledge around the precinct that Kittrell and Quinn were the lead detectives on the recent bank robbery.

Kittrell put his hands on his hips as he surveyed the scene. "What do you think happened here?"

"Looks like a murder-suicide to me," the officer said. "These two guys here were surprised, and then this guy walks over here and shoots himself in the head. Simple as that." He paused. "But I'll let you make the final determination on that."

Kittrell crouched down next to the body of the man who appeared to take his own life. "It doesn't look that simple to me."

CHAPTER 25

REBECCA WESTIN PEERED through her blinds onto an empty street early on Saturday morning. Finally, the media that had been hounding her were gone. A sex tape of a prominent city council member was leaked on the Internet, supplanting the Sid Westin story as the one every editor in every medium of journalism wanted. Driven by a gust of wind, a stray candy bar wrapper tumbled along her front yard. It was the only sign that anyone had even been staked out there—and for what? Quick B roll footage on the news? A picture for the tabloids? She smiled knowing that she had given them nothing the entire time they were out there. She'd even managed to sneak out the back for Sid's funeral. And last night, she'd also snuck out to pick up Jonathan Umbert from the airport.

Mason tugged on her shirt from behind, startling her. She darted to the side as she spun around, falling to the ground.

"Mom, are you okay?"

"Oh, I'm fine. I— You just caught me off guard, that's all." She collected herself and then knelt down to get eye level with him. "Are you okay, Mason?"

He shook his head. "I miss Dad."

She pulled him tight and gave him a hug before standing up. "You and me both."

It wasn't a complete lie. She did miss Sid. Surely, she could've done worse when it came to accepting a marriage proposal. After all, Sid had the potential to make a large amount of money, not to mention become famous in the process. While she wished she could've chosen a different path for her life, she quit sulking about her decisions long ago. Instead, she vowed to make new decisions, decisions that could influence her future in a positive way. And though she wasn't proud of what she'd done, her future seemed brighter now. However, she never imagined that she'd actually miss Sid as much as she did.

While she was lost in thought, Mason hadn't moved. She hadn't even noticed him until he sneezed.

"Oh, Mason, you're still here. I didn't even know you were standing right next to me."

"Can I go outside and play? I'm tired of staying inside all the time."

"Sure. Are you going to practice soccer?"

He nodded. "I want to make Dad proud." He started to walk away before he paused and turned around to face his mother. "Do you think Dad can see me playing from Heaven?"

"I'm sure he can. And I'm sure he'll be proud of you out there practicing hard. Go get 'em, little buddy."

A smile flickered across his face as he headed toward the door. The last time she saw one of those on her son's face was when she watched Sid kick the ball with Mason in the front yard the day of his death.

Her phone rang, and she rushed across the room to answer it. The name and accompanying picture flashing on the screen brought a smile to her face as well. It was Jonathan Umbert.

"Well, hey, you. How was the rest of your night last night?"

Umbert didn't return any pleasantries. "Where are you?"

"I'm at home. What's going on? You sound nervous."

"I just checked my messages and had one from a reporter from *The Times*, a Cal Murphy and—"

"Yeah, that jerk wrote some story about me being part of some FBI probe, but I don't believe a word of it."

"Becs, are you crazy? They are going to nail you."

"For what? I didn't do anything."

"Look, I understand if that's how you want to be, but there is something going on here, and you know what you've done. I read about it all this morning. If they're on to Lancaster, you know it's only a matter of time before they're on to you."

"And you, too."

"I can handle myself, but you need to leave—like thirty seconds ago."

"I'm not going anywhere."

"Becs, think about Mason. If you get arrested, who's going to take care of him? And if he's taken, you're crazy if you don't think your assets will be frozen—or perhaps controlled by the state."

"The government could do that?"

"Health and Welfare can do whatever they want if they deem the child is in danger. I know it might be different in England, but here you've got no recourse—especially a single parent with no relatives living here."

"My sister-in-law is here."

"And you're fine with Alicia caring for Mason and

spending all your money while you sit in jail for who knows how long? Pack your bags and get out of the country—now."

Rebecca paused for a moment to think. Everything he said made sense. But she didn't want to leave without him. "What about you? What are you going to do?"

"I'll join you later. I've got to get a few things in order first, but you need to go to a country where there's no extradition treaty so they don't pursue any trumped up charges. You being gone will make this case too costly to pursue."

"So where should we go?"

"I've got just the place."

CHAPTER 26

CAL COLLAPSED ONTO THE COUCH and held a bag of ice on his ribs. If he had a muscle that didn't ache from his invigorating morning run, it hurt from the pounding he took at the hands of the assailant who attacked him in the alleyway after breakfast. He was already starting to miss Kelly, but now he wanted her home twenty minutes ago— even if he knew she'd give him a hard time about being careless. The beating wasn't his fault, but he wondered why no one ever warned him about the Lynch family. Or maybe knowledge of their family's power wasn't well known beyond the docks.

He turned on the television and flipped the channels until he came to some basketball. March Madness had descended upon the rest of America and consumed the lives of sports fans who weren't interested in solving murders. Cal had almost forgotten about the tournament.

Oregon was playing Xavier in a tense second-round matchup, and the outcome appeared destined to be determined by whichever team had the ball for the final possession. For a moment, Cal almost forgot about his injury. He sat up on the couch, rooting against one of his alma mater's rivals. "Come on, Xavier!" he shouted, yet the second he did, he felt a tight twinge in his chest.

He grimaced as he watched the clock begin to tick away. "Come on, Musketeers!"

The sound of his phone buzzing interrupted his intense cheering for the lower-seeded team from Cincinnati. He glanced at the screen and didn't recognize the number.

Who's calling me now?

"Cal Murphy," he said as he answered.

"Mr. Murphy, I'm so glad you picked up."

"Who is this?"

"I'm sorry. My name is Alicia Westin; I'm Sid's sister."

Cal leaned back on the couch. "I'm sorry about your brother, Alicia."

"Thanks. It's been rough on us, but we're getting through it."

Despite wanting to get back to the game, Cal turned the volume down on the television a few notches. Alicia's strong English accent was a small consolation prize for getting interrupted at this point in the game. "So, how can I help you?"

"I noticed you haven't written anything lately on the robbery. In fact, no one has. What's going on?" She kept going without taking a breath. "The Seattle police won't give me any answers by saying they can't talk about an ongoing investigation. It seems odd that they're not interested in the fact that Rebecca kept pestering Sid to up their life insurance. I want some answers."

"Slow down, Alicia. Just slow down. I might be able to help, but I want you to take a deep breath." He waited for a moment until her shallow breathing ceased. "Are you okay now?"

"That depends on what you're about to tell me."

"Before I answer some of your questions and tell you what's going on, I want to know why exactly you feel like your brother's death was a murder. What makes you think that? By all accounts from law enforcement officials, it was an armed robbery gone bad."

"I know that's what it looks like, but I don't think that was really the case. The robbers escaped with a measly two hundred thousand dollars. What four guys would rob a bank for just fifty thousand each? The risk and reward equation seems off."

"Any other reasons?"

"Sid told me about a year ago that Rebecca wouldn't stop bugging him to up their life insurance."

"Is that one of the reasons why he served her divorce papers?"

"No." Alicia paused for a moment. "Rebecca was never interested in my brother really. She just wanted his money, and she used her assets to put him in a trance. I'd been telling him that for years, even before they married. He finally woke up to the truth and realized what he should have a long time ago."

"And you feel like she wanted more money and created a plot to have him killed?"

"Yes. Sid already had a two-million-dollar life insurance policy and, unless he was lying to me, he had quite a healthy bank account through investmenting on the stock market and had more than twenty million. Rebecca would live a comfortable life if something ever happened to him. But she demanded he increase the policy to ten million."

"Uh, huh," Cal said as he scratched down a few notes on a pad. "And you think that extra eight million was the motivation she needed to kill him."

"Maybe. I don't know if he ever actually increased his policy or not. I just remember hearing him complain incessantly about her nagging to get him to do it."

"That's an important fact. If there's any way you can get that—"

"Mr. Murphy, do you think Rebecca's going to tell me that now?"

"I never suggested asking her."

The line went silent for a few seconds. "Oh, are you suggesting what I think you're suggesting?"

"I just asked if there's any way you can get that information. How you get it is up to you. But it sure would be helpful to know that if you're really going to accuse your sister-in-law of a murder-for-hire plot."

"I just can't believe he's gone," she said before breaking down and crying.

Cal grew uncomfortable with her show of emotion. He hated watching his wife cry, but he could almost always do something to comfort her. But a woman he'd recently met over the phone now heaving sobs? Cal realized there was nothing more he could do for her—or nothing more he could learn from her at the moment.

"Again, Alicia, I'm sorry for your family's loss, but I will look into this. I'm no longer the reporter assigned to this story, but I will do my best to explain this to my editor and see what he says."

"You're not the reporter on this story? Why? What happened? Are they trying to shut you out, too? What's really going on here?"

"I can assure you that I'd like to know just as much as you do, but at the moment, my hands are tied. I'm still trying to search out the best direction to go. But trust me, the moment I figure out what that is, I'll give you a call. I'm going to need your help."

"Thank you," she said as she sniffled.

"We can't get discouraged in our fight for justice," Cal said. "The road to justice is often long, bumpy, and uncomfortable—but it's a worthy trip."

"Thank you, Mr. Murphy."

"Please, call me Cal."

"Okay, Cal. Thanks for your help. I won't stop until my brother's murder has been paid for by the person or people who did this."

"You and me both, Alicia."

Cal hung up and set his phone down on the coffee table. He needed to think. Bill Rafferty's raspy voice coming from the surround sound system jarred him. "Onions!" Rafferty shouted as Xavier players danced around the court. "Little fella with the big three when it mattered most!"

At least one good thing happened today.

Cal turned the television off and pondered all the information he'd just taken in. Despite Alicia's desperate plea to have someone investigate Sid's death as a murder, he had to back up and look at what she said objectively. He was her ally in this theory, but it bordered more along the lines of a conspiracy theory due to the glaring lack of evidence. Anything they had was circumstantial at best, plain weird at worst.

The elements appeared to be there, but Cal couldn't construct a theory that had any legs. He felt like he was trying to solve a puzzle and forcing the final pieces into place. Raising his hands and saying done wasn't the way to win people over to his side or even interest them in his ideas about what really happened to Sid Westin. Without hard evidence, Cal was doing nothing more than speculating. And those theories would never see ink in the paper or even pixels on *The Times'* website.

His phone buzzed again, this time with a call from a number he recognized—his favorite source on the inside at Seattle FC, Javier Martinez.

"Javy! How are you, my friend?" Cal said, answering the phone.

"Just getting ready to suit up for our game here in Salt Lake. And you?"

"I've been better."

"I heard about your altercation with Ramsey."

"Who told you?"

Martinez laughed. "Moore told us this morning at our walk through. I think it's great, man. Ramsey's a punk. Nobody on the team likes him."

"I wish my editor felt the same way. Unfortunately, I'm off the story about Sid."

"What? You've gotta be kidding me?"

"I wish I was, but I'll still hear whatever you've got."

"I almost hate to say this now that I know you're not covering this story."

"That could change, depending on what you're about to say."

"Well, it's not even really about the story you've been working on, but I thought it might be of interest to you."

"Go ahead. I'm listening."

"I just found out that Tim Peterson is about to be suspended."

"For what?" Cal said as he prepared to jot down some notes from his conversation.

"For PED usage. He just failed his most recent drug screening; he was using HGH."

"That might have more to do with Sid's death than you know."

CHAPTER 27

KITTRELL FISHED THE WALLET out of the back pocket of the man who appeared to be the aggressor in the scene of the alleged murder-suicide. "Robert Elton Fisher, according to his driver's license," Kittrell said aloud. "Anybody know anything about him?"

He looked up to see officers shaking their heads and mumbling offhand about how Fisher was a relatively small-time criminal.

Kittrell saw something that captured his attention. Fisher's sleeves were rolled up to his elbow. And it was a strange tattoo design that he eyed, demanding a closer look.

What's this?

He grabbed a pair of latex gloves from his pocket and started to roll up Fisher's sleeves to his shoulders.

"Hey, Manny," Kittrell yelled at one of the officers working the scene. "Come here. I want you to look at something for me."

"What is it?" Manny said as he knelt down next to the body.

"You recognize this tattoo?"

"It looks familiar." Manny Romero gazed off into the distance as he tried to recall where he'd seen it. He started to snap his fingers. "I know. I remember now. It's the same tattoo from that gang we busted at the docks two years ago. They were into all kinds of stuff. Extortion, gambling, bribery, drugs, trafficking. If there was something or someone to exploit, they would be found nearby."

"So you didn't get all those guys?"

Manny shook his head. "A few of the ring leaders are still in prison, but most of the grunt workers either got a slap on the wrist, three to six months in the slammer at best."

"You think he was one of the ones you rounded up?"

"Perhaps, but his name isn't ringing a bell." Manny shrugged. "Doesn't mean anything though. I have a hard time remembering what I ate for dinner last night."

Kittrell chuckled and slapped Manny on the arm. "Thanks for the help. And don't announce this as a murder-suicide just yet. Fisher's body is lying in an awkward position."

Manny stood up. "So what happened, oh great crime scene whisperer?"

Kittrell waved off Manny. "I've got a theory—one you'll hear about later once I confirm a few things."

Kittrell took his gloves off and snapped a few more pictures of the scene with his phone. His particular interest centered around Fisher's body. The two other dead cohorts didn't interest him, at least not yet.

As he drove back to the precinct, Kittrell tried to assemble his theory. At the moment, it was weak, but if his hunch proved him correct, he'd be able to make his case and hopefully receive Chief Roman's blessing to pursue the line of investigation. He wasn't certain of anything at this point, but he knew there were enough suspicious elements to this bank robbery case to realize that there was more beneath the surface—perhaps much more than anyone ever imagined.

When he entered the precinct, Kittrell was met by Chief Roman.

"Please tell me I can close this case by telling the press that these greedy sons of bitches all died in a shootout with one another?" Roman said before taking a sip from his coffee. "I'm so tired of everyone crawling all over me about this case."

Kittrell held up his finger as he rushed past Roman. "Not yet."

Roman threw his head back as anguish washed over his face. "I swear, Kittrell, if you're wrong about this, I'm going to have you writing parking tickets on Market Street for the next six months."

Kittrell mumbled something unintelligible. He wasn't listening to Roman—or anyone else, for that matter—all he cared about was looking at the footage from the robbery. A few clicks on his mouse and he was watching the images from the surveillance video on his screen. After fifteen seconds, he saw all he needed to see.

"Sorry, Chief, but you can't close the case yet."

"Please, Kittrell, for the love of God, can you tell me why?"

Kittrell stood up and walked toward his boss as a wry grin eased across his face. "Fisher, the suspect who we think shot and killed both Sid Westin and the security guard, was indeed there at the scene."

"So, it's over? We did it, right?"

Kittrell held up his index finger. "Not so fast, Chief. If you want to close the robbery, fine. Consider it closed. Those three dead bodies at Harrison Street were likely all involved in the robberies. Fisher was wearing the same pair of shoes, and you will likely find that the gun in his hand matched the one fired at the robbery."

"So what's the hold up here?"

Kittrell walked a few steps back toward his desk and tilted his screen toward Roman. The image frozen on the screen was an enlarged and enhanced image of Fisher.

"What am I looking at here?" Roman asked.

"Fisher was left handed." He pointed at the screen. "See. He's waving his gun around with his left hand." Kittrell clicked the mouse and the security video from the bank moved forward, depicting Fisher shooting Sid Westin and then the security guard. "At the scene on Harrison Street, he's holding the gun in his right hand—and the entry wound from the bullet to his head is from the right side."

"So maybe he didn't commit suicide. Maybe it was a shootout and he got shot in the head."

"Nice theory, Chief, but I know that's more wishful thinking on your part than good police work. And I inspected the gunshot wound to Fisher's head. It was from point blank range. No way a shot from across the room created an entry wound like the one I found."

"So, what's your theory, hot shot?"

"I think someone who Fisher knew and trusted was there with them. Whoever our mystery man was made quick work of the other two guys before shooting Fisher."

"Someone he knew and trusted?"

"Someone he trusted very well. Someone he trusted with his life." Kittrell paused to let the theory sink in with Roman. "This was a cover-up job. You can celebrate catching Sid Westin's killer if you like, but there's more to this case—a lot more."

CHAPTER 28

CAL DIALED BUCKMAN'S NUMBER and crossed his fingers. With the way Buckman dismissed him from covering the story after Ramsey leaked edited footage of their altercation, he considered getting back on the story a long shot—but he had to try. Cal's ace in the hole of outing Ramsey as the Emerald City King would only make him look petty and certainly wouldn't guarantee that Buckman would give him the story back.

"Don't you ever take any time off?" Buckman groused after he answered his phone. "I figured you'd be watching basketball somewhere."

"If there's one thing you've taught me, it's that good reporters never sleep on a big story."

Buckman chuckled. "Problem for you is you don't have one right now."

"Maybe you'll disagree with me after what I'm about to tell you."

"I'm listening."

"I just got a call from one of my sources who told me that Seattle FC's Tim Peterson is about to be suspended for PED usage. He tested positive for HGH."

"Oh, drug tests and pro sports, the gift that keeps on

giving. When are these leagues just going to say, 'Screw it. Put whatever you want in your body. See if we care?'"

"Aren't they pretty much already doing this with the exception of an occasional suspension of some no-name player as a show of good faith?"

"You've got a point."

"Do I have my story back?"

"Cal, we've already been through this. What you did to Ramsey was deplorable—assaulting a fellow co-worker and—"

"Assault is such a strong word. Besides, I wasn't the only one throwing punches."

"Whatever. The point is you knew better, and I've got a competent journalist who can take this story from here."

Cal sighed. "Maybe next time I'll think twice about passing along my scoops."

"I'd rather you think twice about punching a co-worker."

"Oh, admit it, Buckman. You'd love to punch Ramsey's smug face."

"Wanting to do something and actually doing it are what separates a civilized society from a criminal one. We don't live in the Wild West any more, Cal. You need to learn a lesson."

"Fine. You win. I've learned my lesson. But you know Ramsey's gonna screw it up. Don't act like he's going to be able to deliver this for you and meet your high standards."

"Well, at least he's not punching anyone in the face. I'll take what small concessions I can with him for now."

"Speaking of getting punched in the face, I wanted to let you know I got assaulted in an alley yesterday."

Buckman was quiet for a moment. "Are you okay?"

"I think so. Just a few bruised ribs."

"Glad it was nothing worse. What was it about?"

"Apparently, somebody named William Lynch didn't like the fact that I insinuated that his son used performance enhancing drugs."

"So, he had someone beat you up over that? Seems petty."

"I agree, of course, as do my aching ribs. But that doesn't change what happened. Think you can tell Josh to write a glowing story about him if he wins the game tonight for Seattle FC?"

"This isn't like you, Cal. Normally, you'd want to go after someone who did something like that to you. What's going on?"

"I just need time to plot my revenge."

"Against William Lynch? Good luck with that."

"So, do you want me to go after him or not? I'm getting mixed signals here."

"It's simple: I expect you to go after him, but I wish you wouldn't."

"Again, my ribs agree."

"Well, rest up and don't be stupid—and treat your co-workers better. If you did, you'd be writing a much sexier story."

Cal hung up and let out a frustrated scream over Buckman's position of giving Ramsey this story. His boss had dug his heels in—and justifiably so. But it didn't lessen the pain of knowing that Ramsey was about to steal his scoop and probably win an award or two in the process.

***

EDDIE RAMSEY HUNG UP on his call from Buckman. Cal's misfortune was turning out to be one of his greatest breaks since he'd joined *The Times*. While he secretly admired

Cal professionally, Ramsey remained professionally jealous. He was convinced he was every bit as good of a reporter and writer as Cal Murphy, but he never seemed to get the breaks Cal did—until now. He tried to ignore the fact that his tip, the one that was going to give him the material for an award-winning story, came from Cal by way of Buckman.

Ramsey's job was simple: Get someone close to the Seattle FC front office to confirm the fact that Tim Peterson was about to be suspended by the league for illegal drug use. After that, Ramsey could pad the story with quotes about the FBI investigation into how Rebecca Westin was distributing HGH and let readers connect the dots for themselves. If he could figure out a way to provoke the reader to think that this potentially had something to do with the reason Sid Westin was killed in an armed robbery, all the better. But first things first—getting confirmation about the suspension.

Since Ramsey was devoid of any insider connections on the club—and Buckman wanted to keep his beat reporter as far away from this kind of story as possible—he started by calling the club's media relations director, Paul Holloway.

"Who told you that?" Holloway screamed.

"A credible source," Ramsey answered smugly.

"You need new sources."

"That's not exactly a denial, Paul."

"Do I need to tell you that this team is still grieving the loss of one of its most beloved players? And you're going to pick now to stir the pot?"

"So, that would be a yes then? Peterson is about to be suspended for PED usage?"

"I swear, Eddie, you and Cal Murphy will never get credentials over here again. If I ever see you near our practice facility, I'll have you thrown off the premises for trespassing."

"I'm just doing my job."

"Doing your job, my ass. You think you're going to win the admiration of all your little journalist buddies if you break a big story. But the truth is you're just a hack—and don't you forget it."

The line went dead.

Ramsey set his phone down and stared out the window for a moment. That's when he began to conjure up a conspiracy theory out of little more than a hunch and one emphatic rejection for a confirmation. Either Holloway was being evasive or Cal Murphy was trying to strike back and get Ramsey in trouble with Buckman in retaliation for getting yanked off the story. Ramsey chose to believe his second theory.

He called Buckman back and filled him in on what was happening.

"Well, find another source," Buckman said. "Do you think if you try one guy in the organization that you've performed due diligence? I guarantee you Cal would engage at least fifteen people in a conversation about it before he wrote a story like that—even if the first one confirmed it."

"Yeah. About Cal—I think he's trying to sabotage me. He's just dying to get back on this story."

"Oh, I don't know about that. You've been reading too many conspiracy novels."

"No, I swear. It's true. He did this to set me up. If Holloway sticks to his word and refuses to let me near any of the players, how am I supposed to cover this story? It's going to be a headache—and that's only if we're lucky."

"Hmmm." Ramsey hoped that Buckman was giving pause to consider his theory. Ramsey made sense for once.

"Let me talk to Cal and get a feel for him on this one."

"Great," Ramsey said. "I'll be waiting for your call."

***

CAL COULDN'T BELIEVE BUCKMAN had lost trust in him so easily. If he was honest with himself, he knew he only had himself to blame. He should've never been in that position to begin with. If Kelly had been around to keep him focused, perhaps it never would've happened. He missed her and wished she and Maddie would hurry up and return home. But in the meantime, he had to quit pining and move on. He figured it was only a matter of time before Ramsey screwed something up again, and Buckman might be willing to swallow his pride and get him back on the story.

Speak of the devil!

His phone buzzed with a call from Buckman.

He's probably calling me back to ask me to write the story.

"Buckman, it's like you've got nothing to do on this fine spring afternoon but call me and torture me."

"Save it, Cal. I'm not in the mood right now."

"What's going on?"

"I just got off the phone with Ramsey, and he said that Holloway stoned him on the Peterson story. He wouldn't confirm it for him."

"And you're surprised?"

"Who's your source, Cal? Just let me know so I can have Ramsey confirm with him directly."

Cal took a deep breath, afraid to utter his next few words. "No, Buckman, I'm not gonna do that. I can't break trust with my source. That's the most valuable thing I have right now with anyone I work with." He paused for a moment. "I can't even believe you'd ask me to do that."

"Damn it, Cal. Why are you being so ornery about this?"

"Because this story deserves a pro, not a hack like Ramsey. What did he call, like one person? And then he runs back to you, telling you that everyone is being mean to him?"

Buckman was silent for a few seconds. "If you don't give me your source, I'm going to have to assume that you invented this to get back at Ramsey."

"Wha—How? I can't even believe I'm hearing this."

"And I can't believe that you're acting the way that you are. It's not like you, Cal."

Buckman hung up.

Cal stood up and paced around his living room before letting out a few primal screams. His frustration level had been rising for a while with Buckman and Ramsey—and now he had to release some tension. Before Cal had time to consider the best way to release that tension, his phone rang again, this time with a call from a surprising person: Jonathan Umbert.

"Hi, Cal. I heard that you were looking for me while I was gone," Umbert began. "But I'm back now."

"Where were you again? London?"

"Yes, now I can't discuss details or name names at this point, but it appears like Seattle FC might be getting some fine up and coming talent next season."

"That's not why I stopped by your office."

"Yes, I heard that you were accompanied by a detective. Is everything okay? Is this about Sid? Have the police found anything yet?"

"Not yet, but they're close. I was just consulting with the Seattle PD on the case since I'm no longer covering it."

"Well, just let me know any time. My door is always open."

"How late is it going to be open this evening?"

"Well, I'm just going to be down here watching some basketball on the big screen in my office and catching up on some paperwork. Feel free to stop by this evening if you like."

"I'll call you when I'm headed your way."

Cal hung up and dashed over to his laptop. He had an idea but needed to confirm it. He quickly called up the documents he'd received from the FBI regarding Dr. Bill Lancaster and the HGH distribution allegations. He remembered that there were a number of players in the Seattle area who were the supposed recipients of the illegal drugs. However, Cal had never been able to make a common connection. Initially, he suspected that maybe it was a doctor who consulted with the all the city's pro sports teams. But there wasn't one. Then he wondered if it was a sports medicine doctor who worked with athletes who'd been injured or maybe even a therapist. Yet in his cursory research, he couldn't find any connections.

Then he stopped and started typing the name of each athlete listed in the report and researching them again. With each name, he began to realize a common denominator.

A smile spread across his face.

Gotcha!

He picked up his phone and dialed Kittrell's number.

"Wait until he hears this."

CHAPTER 29

CAL DIDN'T HESITATE to put his basketball viewing on hold. He was already so far behind in *The Times*' office pool that he was sure Sandra in accounting might have a legitimate claim on his job by the end of the tournament. He drove toward Umbert's downtown office, which happened to be only a few blocks away from the Seattle PD's main precinct.

Parked in the garage, Cal waited for Kittrell. After a few minutes of listening to the end of the game between Duke and Purdue, Cal shielded his eyes when Kittrell rolled into the parking spot next to him. He got out of his car and waited for Kittrell to do the same.

"You ready?" Cal asked as Kittrell climbed out of his car.

"Let's nail this bastard."

They entered the elevator and stood quietly before Kittrell broke the silence.

"Cal, don't you write a word of this—not until you run this by me. You understand? I can't have Chief looking bad."

Cal nodded. "Got it."

The front desk in the spacious decadent office was unoccupied.

"He should really spend more on hiring dedicated employees," Kittrell said, sarcasm dripping in his tone. "What kind of agent doesn't have a secretary working on Saturday afternoon during March Madness? This is a disgrace."

They both continued to scan the office before Umbert stumbled out of a pair of glass doubles and into the lobby.

"Welcome, you two," Umbert said as he spread his hands wide. "I appreciate you making your way down here to talk about this little issue."

"Little issue?" Kittrell bellowed. "We're talking about an investigation into what quite possibly was murder, Mr. Umbert. And for one of your clients, no less. Show some respect."

Umbert offered his hand toward the detective. "Detective Mel Kittrell, I presume?"

Reluctantly, Kittrell took Umbert's hand and shook it without a word.

"I apologize for not being more respectful of the dead, but I can assure you that I have nothing but respect for Sid Westin. He was one of my first clients when I relocated to the Northwest—and one of my best clients, too."

Kittrell stared at Umbert as their eyes locked. Cal, who stood to Kittrell's right, understood Umbert's tone even more so than his words. It was clear that Umbert was laying the groundwork for what would be his defense: Sid Westin was far more valuable to him alive than dead. Kittrell didn't appear to be fazed by the first haymaker landed in what was shaping up to be a tense meeting.

"Gentlemen, let's proceed inside and get this interview over with," Cal said. He wasn't used to playing peacemaker but realized it was suddenly a necessary role.

"Shall we?" Umbert said, pivoting and gesturing toward the glass doors behind him.

The three men entered the office. Umbert, who brought

up the rear, voiced directions that led them to the conference room located at one corner of the building. The room yielded a spectacular view of the city, which started to twinkle as dusk slowly gave way to night.

"I like to come up here and think," Umbert said. "Nothing like a glorious vista to spark the imagination."

"Or hatch a murder plot," Kittrell said as he spun around and glared at Umbert.

"Detective, I can assure you that I have nothing to hide because I've done nothing wrong."

Kittrell pulled out the chair at the head of the conference room table and sat down. "I'll be the judge of that."

CHAPTER 30

MATT NORFOLK LACED UP HIS CLEATS as he glanced around the Seattle FC locker room. Most of the players were getting ready by going through their pre-game rituals, consisting of everything from reading the Bible to jamming to heavy metal through a pair of ear buds to playing a ukulele. There was a little bit of something for everyone. But today was different. Norfolk couldn't help but feel a twinge of loss since Sid Westin wasn't next to him. They'd always been put next to each other in the locker room for as long as he'd been on the squad. Instead, Tim Peterson occupied the small space next to him.

Norfolk stared at Peterson, whose pregame ritual included eating an apple and reading a copy of GQ magazine. Yet Peterson had his head buried in his hands.

"Cheer up, mate," Norfolk said. "Just because you're in the dead man's locker doesn't mean you're next."

Eyes narrowing, Peterson turned slowly toward Norfolk. "I'm not in the mood, Peterson."

"How about you get your mind on the game because it's clearly elsewhere."

Shawn Lynch walked by their locker and overheard the conversation. He tapped Norfolk on the shoulder. "Go easy on him, Norfolk. He just found out he's been suspended for using PEDs."

Norfolk leaned back, mouth agape. "Wow, Peterson. If you're using PEDs, you ought to at least look like you take them."

Peterson didn't say a word, instead choosing to let his fists do the talking. He took a wild swing at Norfolk that landed on his chin. Caught off guard, Norfolk crashed to the floor. He felt his face for blood before getting to his knees. But instead of standing up, Norfolk lunged at Peterson's knees. Despite giving up forty pounds to Norfolk, Peterson quickly escaped Norfolk's grasp and took the more advantageous position. He'd often bragged about his three state championship titles in wrestling while he was in high school, but the rest of the team mocked his claim since he was from Montana, and they joked that he only had to beat one other wrestler to win it. But nobody was laughing now.

Peterson wrapped his arms around Norfolk's head and started to apply pressure.

"I bet you're the one who did this to me," Peterson said.

"Did what?" Norfolk said as he struggled to escape Peterson's grasp.

"You took your drug test the same time as me. You switched them."

"That's insane. How could I have done that? Besides I've never used any PEDs."

Peterson released him, but it appeared only to be a tactical move.

"I watched you buy a Screwball from the ice cream truck at the Shawnmon Bay Park every week. You think I don't know what's going on here? You think I don't know what's going on with some of the people on this team?" Peterson glared around the room.

"I swear, Tim-Bo. You gotta believe me. I had nothing to—" Norfolk said before he went limp.

Peterson let go of Norfolk, who'd been put to sleep. He stood up and walked around the room, eyeing each one of his teammates closely. "I know each one of you who is involved in this mess. And you better believe I'm going to make sure you all go down with me."

Javier Martinez walked over to Peterson and took him by the arm, whispering in his ear. "Calm down, man. It's okay. I believe you."

CHAPTER 31

KITTRELL LEANED BACK in his chair and tapped his pen on his notebook. "I have to be honest with you, Mr. Umbert, this doesn't look good for you. We have a mountain of evidence pointing in your direction."

Umbert shifted in his seat before he began to make his plea. "Why on earth would I possibly kill off one of my biggest cash cows? Sid Westin was hooking me up with a substantial amount of money each year off his contract. It doesn't make sense."

"Where were you on Thursday?" Kittrell asked.

"I was in London, checking out a prospective client. I already told you that."

"Can anyone corroborate your story?"

"Just look on social media. You'll see pictures of me in London during that time. There's no way I could've faked that."

Kittrell stared out the window at the dark sky and took a deep breath before continuing, "Since you have so much money, Mr. Umbert, perhaps you hired someone to take care of some business for you while you were away."

"This is absurd."

"It's not as absurd as you wish," Kittrell said as he

opened a folder in front of him. "Are you aware that the FBI is investigating Rebecca Westin in an alleged doping scheme with a—" Kittrell glanced at his notes—"Dr. Bill Lancaster?"

"I read the paper."

"I'll take that as a yes."

"What does this have to do with Sid Westin's death and that bank robbery?"

"I was hoping you could tell us."

"Seriously, I have no idea what you're talking about. A client of mine is dead, gunned down senselessly in an armed robbery, and his wife is being investigated by the FBI in a doping scheme—yet you question me, as if I had anything to do with all this."

"Speaking of connections, Mr. Umbert, I believe your connection to the Westin family is far greater—and far more complicated—than you're letting on."

"Please, Detective. Just spit it out."

Kittrell grabbed a half-dozen sheets and slid them across the table to Umbert. "Any of these look familiar?"

Umbert remained stoic, unflappable in the presentation of the proof he demanded to see. "So maybe Rebecca and I had a fling. It proves nothing."

Kittrell shook his head. "Except, it proves everything, creating a definitive link and establishing a potential motive."

"A link to what?"

Kittrell motioned to Cal. "Show him what you found."

Cal slid a piece of paper to Umbert. It was the link he established and had been so excited to tell Kittrell about. This evidence would be damning in court. "Every name given to us by the FBI just so happens to be a client of yours. Coincidence? I think not."

Umbert clenched his fists so hard that they started to turn white. "This doesn't prove anything. I represent over half of the pro athletes in the city. And almost all of them are the marquee players."

Rain started to pelt the windows.

Kittrell held up his finger. "It doesn't, except I can easily establish a believable motive. You had the means and a strong motive."

"What is that? Kill off Sid Westin so I can have Rebecca?" Umbert looked away from Kittrell. "I already have her. Why would I need to kill her husband? Granted, I'm a slow learner, but after my second wife depleted me of most of my assets, I vowed never to marry again. And that's one vow I intend to keep."

"But I suspect Sid found out about what you were doing—both to his wife and with his wife. And he was going to turn you in."

"You know, Detective, I think we're done here. If you want to continue this conversation, I prefer to do it with my lawyer present. I tried to do this as a favor for you, but I didn't realize you were going to try and ambush me with a murder accusation." Umbert stood up and gestured toward the door.

Kittrell got up slowly as he collected his evidence and re-inserted it into the folder. "Sid Westin found out that his wife was in bed with you both figuratively and literally, and he threatened to turn you in."

"I appreciate your fervor in solving this case because Sid was not only a client but a friend, and—"

"Friends don't sleep with their friends' wives."

"—and I hope you catch the killer. Sid deserves justice."

"You're a brazen hypocrite, Mr. Umbert," Kittrell fired

back, turning toward the exit. "And I'm going to put you where you belong."

"Good luck with that, Detective."

"I don't need luck. Just a little more proof." He hit Umbert gently with his folder. "No more trips out of the country, you hear? You stick around Seattle until this is all cleared up."

Umbert flashed a faint smile. "Yeah, I hear extradition can be a bitch sometimes."

CHAPTER 32

CAL FOLLOWED KITTRELL as he stormed outside the building and let a string of expletives fly. The rain had subsided, but the accompanying wind hadn't. The stiff breeze caught Cal off guard, and he staggered to his left under the force of it.

Neither man said a word for a few moments as they stewed on their interaction with Umbert. There was little doubt that he was guilty, but proving so would be a difficult matter, and Cal could see Kittrell's frustration mounting along with the pressure to solve the case.

"What did Umbert mean by his comment about extradition? You think he's toying with us?"

Kittrell put his hands behind his head and paced around in circles. He sighed before he answered, "I think he's taunting us, for sure. But if we can't get some physical evidence that ties him to the robbers, we're just dealing with circumstantial evidence and hunches. The DA wouldn't move to prosecute such a weak case, especially against a man who has a lot of connections among the wealthy and powerful."

"So, tell me what we need."

"We need to know what Sid Westin knew before he was killed, and if he knew anything at all. That would be a start.

And this appears like a classic murder-for-hire plot. So, we'd need to be able to track a large payment from Umbert to somewhere else. And I doubt we'll ever find that. Umbert isn't stupid."

"What you're saying then is that he pulled off the perfect murder?"

"Perfect in that he's never going to go to jail a day in his life if we don't find something."

Cal put his hands on his hips and watched the flags in the plaza in front of the building thrash violently. It's how he'd felt the entire time chasing down this story. And coming so close to apprehending the person responsible for Sid's death without acquiring prosecutable evidence felt painfully empty.

"Do you think there's anything I could do to help regarding a story in the paper?" Cal asked.

Kittrell sighed. "I don't think so. We're probably better off gathering all our hard evidence before making another run at Umbert. I wanted to serve notice to him that we're onto him. Maybe he'll make a mistake. But at this point, there's nothing you can do. I think a story would do more harm than good."

"Okay, I'll keep this quiet."

"Yeah, don't tell your editor."

***

ON HIS DRIVE HOME, Cal called his FBI contact and friend, Agent Jarrett Anderson. Cal wanted to see if there was any more to the story about Dr. Lancaster that he leaked—and if maybe there was another story Anderson wanted to give him. Anything to avoid covering boat races on a Sunday.

"I don't have anything else new I can release at this point," Anderson said. "However, I can tell you that we're close to creating a case against Rebecca Westin. One of our undercover agents captured video of her giving packages directly to a few players we've identified straight out of a van."

"A white van?"

"Yeah—it was fronting as an ice cream truck. Pretty slick operation, if you ask me. I mean, other than the obvious question of 'Why is a professional athlete's wife driving an ice cream truck?'"

"It is a rather odd side job, isn't it?"

"But what gets me is why Sid would've purchased a van in the first place. It's an even stranger choice for an extra vehicle."

Cal came to a stop at a traffic light. "I did some digging into that myself because I was asking the same question."

Anderson's voice quickened, "And what'd you find?"

"Sid liked to volunteer at an inner city program that often needed help moving families. He bought a work van because it was more versatile than a truck, according to the guy he bought it from. And my guess is that Rebecca saw a creative opportunity and took it."

"Did she admit she knew about the van?"

"No. She claims she didn't even know it existed. But I happen to know now that her partial prints were all over it, based off a forensics report I peeked at."

"I thought those didn't come up with any matches."

"Not in our database. But they came up when we did a cross agency search and found them in a European database."

"Thanks for the info. We're very close to busting her. It won't be good publicity for the bureau to do it right now after her husband was killed, but we won't wait long to act. We still have a few more details to take care of in the meantime. When we charge someone, we almost always get a conviction."

Cal eased onto the gas as the light turned green. "You'll keep me in the loop when you do, right?"

"Of course, Cal. Your help has been invaluable in getting us what we need to secure a conviction. Your story forced her to have some interesting conversations with Jonathan Umbert. Good thing we had a wiretap beforehand, or we might have missed some of their conversations."

"Thanks, Anderson. I appreciate it."

"Not sure I'll ever be able to repay you for helping us rescue Noah Larson's son, but I'll keep trying."

"If that's what you're trying to do, that's your own self-imposed debt, not mine. We're good as far as I'm concerned. But I do appreciate the tips."

"Any time, Cal."

Cal hung up and pulled into his driveway. He waited for the garage door to open when he received an incoming call from his wife.

"Please tell me you're coming home soon," Cal began. "I miss you guys terribly."

Kelly laughed. "Running out of clean underwear, are we?"

"The dishes are piled high in the sink, if you must know." Cal chuckled. "I'm kidding. No, I only miss you and Maddie."

"Well, I'm here to tell you that your wish is my command. The Charlotte airport is running at full strength tomorrow, and we've got tickets for a flight back to Seattle."

"Outstanding. When are you getting in?"

"Late. I'll text you the times." She paused. "Have you been staying out of trouble?"

Cal carefully considered his response before speaking. He wanted to be honest without causing alarm. "For the most part."

"Cal!"

"Just a minor incident. I got roughed up in an alleyway."

"You got beat up?"

"Beat up is such a strong way of describing what happened."

"Assaulted?"

"Even stronger."

"Well, what happened?"

"Nothing too major. Just got kicked in the ribs a few times."

"By who?"

Cal sighed. "I'm not sure. The guy wore a mask and was gone before I could get a good look at him, but I think he works for William Lynch."

"The Cars, Cars, Cars guy?"

"The one and only."

"Why would he do that to you?"

"Apparently, he didn't like how I insinuated that his son, Shawn, who plays for Seattle FC, was possibly using PEDs in my article."

"People are so touchy these days."

Cal broke into laughter. Kelly's deadpan humor often caught him off guard, though it shouldn't have after being married to her for a few years. "Well, I'm all right, and I doubt he'll mess with me again unless I write a nasty article about Shawn. And if Buckman holds his ground with me, it certainly won't happen any time soon."

"Well, don't write anything tonight that will get you in trouble, and we'll see you tomorrow."

Cal hung up and watched a few minutes of highlights on SportsCenter before getting ready for bed. He turned over theory after theory, hoping to figure out some way that Kittrell could pin Sid's death on Umbert. But nothing. Cal figured he might have a better opportunity in the morning after he'd had a solid night of sleep.

***

ONCE HIS ALARM CLOCK went off and jarred him awake, Cal threw on a hat, grabbed his keys, and left the house in search of a good breakfast. He'd been so consumed with getting to the restaurant that he hadn't seen the multiple text message alerts from Kittrell. He turned on the radio and caught the sports news update on KJR.

The biggest story of the day—and perhaps the year so far—revolves around a report in today's edition of *The Times*, regarding former Seattle FC star Sid Westin and his agent Jonathan Umbert. According to the paper's sources, Umbert is a prime suspect in a strange murder-for-hire plot that resulted in Westin's death.

"Are you kidding me?" Cal yelled at the radio as he turned it off. A wave of emotions swept over him, starting with anger and rage followed by betrayal and embarrassment. He glanced at his phone again, afraid to listen to the voice messages from Kittrell.

After he pulled into the restaurant parking lot, Cal played the messages. Both of them were scathing rebukes, sent minutes apart. Kittrell's first message would've sufficed, but Cal didn't blame him for leaving a second one, just in case the first one wasn't clear enough. He deleted both messages and then called Buckman.

"Why didn't you tell me about this story?" Cal demanded.

"Cal, are you that dense or just stupid?" Buckman asked. "Let me break this down for you as clearly as possible: You're not on the story. Ramsey is—and he got a tip from one of his contacts at the precinct last night about what was going down."

"I knew what was going down."

"Congratulations. But you weren't on the story, so it doesn't matter."

"I was there and witnessed the interrogation."

"And you didn't call me to tell me about it?"

"I promised not to since I'm serving as a special consultant on this case with Detective Kittrell."

"Doesn't he have a partner?"

"He does, but he's sick this week, so I've been filling in. And part of my deal was that I couldn't write about any of this until I got the green light from him."

"Well, look on the bright side," Buckman started, "you didn't write it, and you won't be for a long time."

"He's going to think I'm his source."

"Tell him it was someone else but you don't know who. And if he wants to know who it was, he can figure it out. He's a detective, isn't he?"

"This isn't going to be bode well for my future with any of the officers over there."

"Good thing you're not covering the police beat for the paper then, right? Besides, I'm sure you'll find a way to patch things up and move forward."

Cal rubbed his face with both hands and growled. He

wanted to blame Ramsey or Buckman—or better yet, punch something. But he knew it was his fault. Letting his temper get the best of him was what got him into this situation in the first place. Without that incident with Ramsey, none of this would've ever happened.

His phone buzzed again, this time with a call from Kittrell.

Cal moaned and answered, bracing to get an earful from the detective. Kittrell didn't disappoint.

"How could you? I trusted you, Cal. I just can't believe you would do that to me. I've been on the phone with Chief Roman for the past half hour while he ripped me a new one. I just can't—"

"I know this might be hard for you to believe, but it wasn't me," Cal said, interrupting Kittrell's rant. "I swear. I would never break your trust like that. You've gotta believe me."

"I don't have to believe anything. We discussed this. I brought you on to help with this case under the condition that you wouldn't write anything without my prior consent. But it's apparent that you just used me to get a story."

"If you only knew how much I despise Eddie Ramsey, you'd realize your latest statement was laughable. That guy exists to give journalists a bad name."

"Oh, I doubt they need much help."

"Look, I'm sorry this happened, but I promise you I had nothing to do with it."

Kittrell didn't seem interested in Cal's apology. "You wanna know what the worst thing is about all this?" It wasn't a question. "Rebecca Westin got on a plane last night headed for Dubai. And in case you're not up on your extradition treaties, there isn't one for the UAE. She's in the wind now.

And if you think I'm upset, wait until you hear from your friends over at the FBI about this."

Kittrell ended the call, and Cal was left to ponder how everything seemed to be unraveling all at once. Not only had Ramsey's story set back the Seattle PD's ability to catch the person behind Sid Westin's death, it had also severely damaged Cal's relationship with Kittrell and the rest of the police department.

Cal took a deep breath and remained in his car. He needed to think of something—and fast.

CHAPTER 33

KITTRELL POURED ANOTHER CUP of coffee and tried to calm down. He noticed his hand shaking as he started to type on his keyboard. The caffeine? Rage? He wasn't sure why. As this case wore on, he needed to have a clear head to decipher how to navigate this investigation. Obviously, his plan to loop in a consultant had failed.

Chief Roman rumbled past his desk before stopping and turning around. "Look, I know I was hard on you earlier. I just wanna catch the sonofabitch who did this—and I know you do, too. Focus on the murder-suicide at the garage, and see what comes up. We might not be able to pin this on Umbert, but he might not be the only one involved. It might go higher up than him."

Kittrell nodded, his body language betraying his level of confidence. He'd been through every possible piece of evidence, and no potential lead seemed promising.

After several minutes of sifting through evidence and coming up with nothing new, Kittrell received an email. It was the manifest for the flight Umbert claimed to be on, except his name wasn't on it. Kittrell immediately called the airline back and requested the manifests for all flights originating from London and arriving in Seattle over the past three days. Fifteen minutes later, he had them in his inbox.

Would you look at that?

According to the manifest with Umbert's name on it, Delta Flight 179 landed in Portland around noon on Friday. The coroner's report put the time of death in the supposed murder-suicide off Harrison Street at around 10 PM on Friday.

Why that little liar!

Kittrell hustled down the hall to Chief Roman's office. "Chief, I think I've got something."

Roman looked up from his work. "What is it?"

"Umbert told us that he didn't come in until Saturday afternoon, which would've given him a great alibi. But instead of taking him at his word, I looked into it. He showed me his ticket, but I double-checked with the airline just to make sure. Get this: Turns out he was never on the flight. He flew in a whole day earlier and was here by noon on Friday. According to the coroner's report, the time of death was round 10 PM on Friday which—"

Roman slapped his desk. "Which means that Umbert would've been here in plenty of time. So we've got motive, opportunity, and no alibi. The DA is gonna love you."

Kittrell smiled for the first time in several days. "Yes, he is."

"Now, you want any help bringing him in? I'll gladly stand in for Quinn on this one."

"Nah. I'll handle it."

Kittrell strode down the hallway. He hadn't had that much pep in his step since he convinced Tara in accounting to join him for drinks one night after work.

He only hoped his happiness lasted longer than his date with Tara had.

CHAPTER 34

REBECCA WESTIN TIGHTLY HELD Mason's hand as they wandered through the Dubai International Airport. The men adorned in white robes and red-and-white shemaghs appeared almost as ghosts hovering slowly along. Rebecca felt self-conscious, obviously out of place in this strange structure where the ancient and modern collided. Hathoric columns supported a ceiling that soared above them, while men stood like statues riding moving sidewalks. As a transplant to America, she knew the feeling of entering a foreign culture, but this felt more like entering another galaxy.

She pulled Mason closer and was able to find a taxi with little trouble. Within half an hour, they were checking into the Atlantis hotel at The Palm just before 7 PM Sunday local time. The hotel was gaudy and extravagant, and even with her hefty bank account, she felt slightly guilty for indulging herself like this, especially so soon after Sid's death.

It's for Mason, she tried to convince herself. This will be good for him. He needs this.

The truth is she wanted this. She was the one who needed to escape the fish bowl she'd been living in for the past week or so. Getting out from beneath the scrutinizing, the whispers, the mystery, the tragedy—this was the place to do it. Here, she could be anonymous. Of course, hundreds of other places would've sufficed, but when Umbert called her and told her to book a flight for Dubai, she didn't protest for even a moment. He told her it'd be all right and that they would reunite once everything died down. But she wasn't so sure.

While Rebecca checked in at the registration desk, Mason gawked at an aquarium teeming with exotic fish and other sea creatures.

"Mum! Check this out!" he yelled.

She smiled and waved at him. It was the first genuine moment of happiness she'd experienced in a while. For weeks—even months—leading up to this time, her life felt like a rollercoaster without any ups. It was just one massive downward spiral. For once, life flickered within her through watching her son. His eyes widened as he stared at a stingray hovering near the glass, appearing to be as interested in Mason as Mason was in it.

This is going to be great.

She got her keycard and grabbed their bags, and an attendant hustled over to help. She politely refused his help and called for Mason. He didn't budge.

"If you think that's cool, Mason, just wait until you get to swim with the dolphins," she said.

Immediately, Mason's trance was broken as he spun and ran toward her.

"Dolphins? Real life dolphins? I can swim with them?" he asked.

She nodded. "First thing in the morning."

Mason grabbed his bag and joined her, keeping pace with his mother's long strides.

But they didn't make it to the elevators before she heard a sound that made her cringe. A click-click-click and a loud voice in a British accent.

"That's Rebecca Westin!"

She glanced over her shoulder to see a small contingent of European photographers rushing toward her. She couldn't see who was the subject of their original impromptu photo session, but she didn't look long enough to identify the person—nor did she care. She had become their next target.

Pecking at the elevator button to close the door, she grabbed Mason's hand and told him to look away.

"Come on, come on," she said.

"What is it, Mum? Who are those people?"

"Just keep your head down."

Rebecca couldn't imagine any doors possibly taking longer to close. With her head still down and her eyes shielded by her hand, she looked up ever so slightly to sneak a peek at the oncoming photographers. They were still at least ten meters away as the last glimmer of light from the lobby vanished behind the elevator doors.

She exhaled and tousled Mason's hair. "It's okay now. They're gone."

He looked up at her. "Does this mean we won't be able to swim with the dolphins tomorrow?"

"Nothing is going to stop that. Don't you worry."

He smiled again and squeezed her hand.

***

AFTER REBECCA PUT MASON to bed, she ordered up a bottle of chardonnay from room service. She needed to unwind after a long day of travel, and finding a comfortable stool at the bar wasn't an option tonight.

As she popped the cork, she poked her head into Mason's room. She felt guilty about splurging for a two-room suite, but at fifteen hundred a night for one room, she figured another five hundred wasn't a big deal. Besides, it was only for a few nights. Jonathan Umbert was going to let her know what to do next. Perhaps everything would've died down by now. Surely the feds weren't going to go after her. They'd never have enough evidence to prove anything. As long as Dr. Lancaster kept fastidious records, she would be fine—at least that's what everyone told her. But she didn't want to risk it, especially if it meant losing Mason.

Mason didn't move when the light from the hallway spilled into his room. She could almost see a half smile on his face as he breathed steadily.

She closed the door and meandered out onto the deck. It was still warm—hot by Seattle standards—this late at night. An intermittent breeze off the gulf waters helped cool the air. When the latest gust ended, she tucked her hair behind her ears and leaned on the railing overlooking the palatial grounds of the Atlantis. It was perfect—almost.

Rebecca wanted the man who'd made this moment of freedom possible to join her. And if he couldn't be there in person, the least she could do was call him.

She glanced at her phone. It was a few minutes past midnight in Dubai, which meant it was around 1 PM in Seattle. She dialed Umbert's number. Straight to voice mail.

Undaunted, she called Umbert's assistant, Ellie Dunaway.

"Ellie, this is Rebecca Westin. Do you happen to know where Jonathan is?" she asked as soon as Ellie answered.

"Oh, Mrs. Westin, I'm so sorry to hear about your loss. You're definitely in my thoughts these days."

"Thanks, Ellie." She forced herself to thank the woman even though she knew Ellie didn't mean it. "Now, do you know where Jonathan is by chance? When I called, I went straight to voice mail."

"Oh, you haven't heard?"

"Heard what?"

"It's all over the news."

"Ellie, I'm in Dubai. It's not on the news here."

"Sorry, Mrs. Westin. He's been arrested for murder—and they're saying he killed the men he hired to kill Sid. I'm sorry to tell you like this, but I thought you would've heard this by now."

"Can you tell me any more details?"

"The story on the news is that the bank robbers who killed Sid were all found dead in a warehouse in what first appeared to be a murder-suicide. But then they found out that Mr. Umbert arrived on a flight early enough to kill the men and stage a murder-suicide."

"Did they say when he got back?"

"Yeah, they said sometime around 10 PM on Friday."

Rebecca hung up and smashed her wine glass on the balcony. She let out a frustrated scream and was heading inside when she heard a voice that arrested her attention.

"I know that scream," said an elderly woman on the balcony next to Rebecca's room.

Rebecca stopped and shot the woman a look. "You don't know anything about me."

"I know that when a woman breaks a wine glass, it can only ever be about one thing."

"And what's that?" Rebecca snarled.

"A man."

Rebecca was angry, and she found a target practically

begging to be peppered with multiple rounds of hateful words. "Well, congratulations, Dear Abby. Women only get upset about two things: men or their kids. You had a 50-50 shot."

"And is this man here with you?"

"I didn't ask for a counseling session."

"Good because I'm not giving one. I only give guidance. And if you love this man as much as I think you do, you need to go to this man."

"Not so easy, oh great wise one. He's in prison now."

The old woman didn't flinch. "All the more reason to go to him." She took a long pull on her glass of wine. "I don't know why you're still standing here."

Rebecca's anger yielded to sorrow as she began to sob. She wasn't sure if it was the alcohol or the emotions of everything finally hitting her at once—or a combination of the two. Regardless of the reason, she couldn't stop the tears once they started.

"There you go," the old woman said. "Just let it out. Have a good cry. And then go get your man."

Rebecca didn't say anything for at least a minute. She broke the silence by muttering, "Thank you," to her friendly neighbor and going inside. As much as the woman dishing unsolicited advice bothered Rebecca, she knew the woman was right.

Jonathan Umbert needed her—and her alibi. And he needed her thirty seconds ago.

CHAPTER 35

CAL CAUTIOUSLY APPROACHED THE FRONT STEPS to his house. Something didn't feel right—and it didn't look right either. The doormat was off kilter, and the door was ajar. For a fleeting moment, he thought Kelly and Maddie had taken the redeye home and were trying to surprise him. But he dismissed that idea, concluding that they would've called to check on him if he wasn't there when they arrived.

No, something was wrong.

He pushed the door open slowly.

"Hello?" he said. "Is anybody here?"

There could've been a handful of guys who were playing a prank on him, but he doubted it. Then he considered for a moment that maybe Kelly had asked their cleaning service to come by, knowing he would've kept the house a wreck. And, sadly, she was right.

If this had been his bachelor days, he would've had a hard time proving anyone had been in his house aside from the open door. But Kelly kept their home orderly, and there was no doubt someone had ransacked his house.

As he surveyed the carnage, nothing looked broken or damaged. And nothing seemed to be missing, either. If this was a robbery, it hadn't gone well. Cal figured either the burglar got spooked or the purpose behind the break-in was to scare him. If what really happened was the latter, the robber failed. Such minor incidents were far more common occurrences than Cal preferred—and it didn't faze him.

But it did make him angry.

After he picked up for a few minutes, he sat down at his kitchen table and tried to think about the why.

Why would they target me? Something I wrote? Something I have?

The only person who could possibly be upset enough at something he wrote to strike back would be Rebecca Westin—and she was out of the country. Not that she would do something like this herself. He figured she would've hired somebody for the job. But he doubted someone as vindictive as she was would have his place tossed just to prove a point.

Then there were William Lynch's thugs. They'd already used Cal as a punching bag once but seemed to enjoy sending messages. What they sent, Cal received loud and clear. He passed it along to Buckman, who obviously relayed it to Josh Moore. In that morning's paper, Josh's article sang the praises of Shawn Lynch, who scored the game-winning goal with less than two minutes remaining to give Seattle FC the victory.

Cal couldn't think of anyone else who could possibly have it out that bad for him these days.

Maybe a former client or a disgruntled athlete.

Narrowing down that list wouldn't be easy as it numbered in the dozens. But he also doubted they would go through all this trouble just to send a message. Those people would be looking to exact revenge, make it hurt Cal where he was most vulnerable.

Unable to come up with a reasonable theory, he got up to walk through the house again and inspect the damage more closely. He went into his study and found proof that this was indeed a scare tactic. "Mind Your Own Business" was spray painted on the wall in bright red. Cal called Kittrell.

"What do you want?" Kittrell groused as he answered his phone.

"I need to talk to you about something."

"Look, now isn't a good time, Cal. In fact, you might want to get down here to re-write the story one of your reporters already reported on this morning."

"That's not what I need to talk about."

Kittrell ignored him and kept talking. "We got him. Officially booked Jonathan Umbert for murder charges."

"Jonathan Umbert?"

"Don't act so surprised, Cal. You knew this for a while now and couldn't wait to tell someone, anyone. So, you blabbed it to your loudmouth pal, Eddie Ramsey. At least you'll be the one on the humbling end of this story. Everybody will be singing the praises of Ramsey while you shrink into the corner like a wallflower."

"Wait. You're arresting Jonathan Umbert?"

"Do I sound like I'm stuttering? Feigning disbelief is just so—so ... not you."

"Didn't you keep Umbert in custody all night?"

"All night. And he'll never get anything but three squares and a cot for the rest of his life now."

"You've got the wrong guy," Cal said forcefully. "Stop with your endless rant and listen to me." Cal took a deep breath. "I know you're still upset, but I want to assure you that I didn't tell Ramsey—or even anyone who did. He's got another source, a source from your own department. However, I'm not here to bicker over that, and it never was the purpose of my call."

"Well, why did you call me?"

"Someone broke into my home this morning and left me a message in spray paint telling me to mind my own business."

"Can I sign my name to that sage piece of advice?"

"Enough with the wise cracks, Kittrell. This is serious. And if you think Umbert is your guy, I think you're mistaken."

"So, you were also mistaken yesterday?"

"Yes," Cal said, his voice rising several octaves before descending again. "I'm not afraid to admit when I'm wrong, and while I think Umbert may appear to be a likely suspect, maybe even a sketchy agent, I don't think he killed Sid Westin—even though he had a motive and means to accomplish it."

"What makes you so sure it wasn't him?"

"Well, for one, my house just got tossed while I was at breakfast this morning. And Umbert certainly had no hand in that."

"You don't think he could've orchestrated this from prison to plant doubt in your mind?"

Cal shrugged. "Perhaps, but this felt personal, not like some thief playing mind games with me. I'd say it's far more likely that he didn't have anything to do with that."

"Look, I think you're crazy and paranoid right now. But just for your peace of mind, I'll send one of our guys out there to camp outside your house with a nice view of everything from the street. He'll be able to protect you from the dangerous spray painters."

"This isn't a joking matter, Kittrell."

"I'm only telling you this because I promised, but you need to get down here quickly if you want to scoop Seattle with this story. You wouldn't want Ramsey stealing your thunder two days in a row."

By this point, Cal was seething. He hung up and started to search his house for more clues. There had to be something somewhere that let him know what else was really going on.

CHAPTER 36

REBECCA WESTIN SCOOTED next to Mason on his bed, bracing for the painful news she had to deliver. She rubbed his back, gently awakening him. When he rolled over, he opened his eyes for a moment before shutting them again. Then a grin spread across his face.

"So, Mum, can I go swimming with the dolphins today?" he asked, eyes still shut.

Rebecca exhaled and cringed while she decided how to let him down without crushing him.

"Not today, Mason," she said. "In fact, we're going to go back home."

He opened his eyes, which turned sad. His smile gave way to a frown. "So soon? I thought you said I could swim with the dolphins today, and now we're going home? I don't understand."

"You know how I've talked with you about being content?"

He nodded.

"Well, this is a chance for you to practice this. We don't always get what we want in life."

Mason rolled over and burrowed under the covers. "You do."

"Now, Mason, that's not true. I certainly didn't want your father to die."

"You always get your way."

"Look, I'm not going to argue with you about this, but I do need you to get up and get dressed so we can get to the airport. I've got something important to do."

"I thought you said taking me here was important, and it was important for us to get away from everything and have some time together."

"That's important too, but we need to go back to Seattle because I need to do the right thing. And the right thing isn't running away."

Mason pulled the covers down and sat up. "What did you do?"

She started to rub her hand up and down his back again. "I did some things that I'm not proud of, and now it's time to own up to what I did."

"What do you mean?"

"You remember that time I found out you took Elizabeth Stancil's Wonder Woman action figure?"

He nodded.

"And what did I make you do?"

"Take it back and apologize."

"Well, that's kind of what I'm going to have to do. Now get up so we can get on."

***

MONDAY EVENING, REBECCA WALKED into the Seattle PD precinct downtown and demanded to speak to Detective Kittrell. She was led back to his desk where he met her with a shocked looked on his face.

"Surprised to see me, Detective?" she said, offering her hand.

He shook it and gestured for her to have a seat. "I heard that you were out of the country. What brings you back?"

"I heard you've charged Jonathan Umbert with murder, and I came to clear his name."

Kittrell knit his brow and cocked his head to one side. "And how are you going to do that?"

"By giving him an alibi."

"So, are you suggesting you were with him at the time he murdered the three bank robbers who killed your husband? Or were you the one who pulled the trigger?"

She glared at him and shook her head in disgust. "No." She paused and looked down. "He was with me on Friday night. I picked him up from the airport, and we went to a hotel. He was afraid there might be members of the media staked out at his home as well—and I just knew it would cast suspicion on us. Plus I didn't want Mason to have to hear people saying ugly things about me."

"How long were you there?"

"All night. Then early Saturday morning, I took him back to his office."

"And then you just left the country?"

"He called me a little while later and told me to book the first flight I could to get out of here with Mason. He thought the FBI might try to put me away for my association with Dr. Lancaster. Do you know who he is?"

"I'm aware of the story." Kittrell scribbled some notes on his pad and dropped his pen emphatically. "You know I'm going to have to tell the FBI that you were here, right?"

She nodded as a tear streaked down her face. "I know."

"You're a brave woman coming in here like this. I'll talk

to the chief and see if we can get Umbert released." He pushed a pad and pen in front of her. "I need the name of the hotel and a signed statement from you."

"What about Jonathan? Do you think he'll be able to go home today?"

"We'll need to check out your alibi, go through the hotel's security footage and see if everything meshes with our medical examiner's timeline."

"And when it does?"

"We'll likely release him."

She exhaled and forced a smile. "That's all I want. I just couldn't bear the thought of him going to prison for something he didn't do—even if it cost me my freedom." She put her head down and started to write.

After a few moments of silence, Kittrell spoke, "You must really love him."

She stopped and looked up. "I do. I never wanted things to go the way they did with Sid. He was the one who wanted to divorce me—though I wasn't about to put up a fight. The way he was always running around on me … He didn't deserve me, but he didn't deserve to die like that either."

"Do you think someone targeted him?"

She finished her statement and then signed it, pushing it back across the desk toward Kittrell. "I guess we'll never know now, will we? With those robbers all dead, there's not much point in pursuing it, is there?"

"Don't you want closure—and justice?"

"I got closure when he served me with those papers. As for justice? Does justice ever really accomplish anything for the victims or the perpetrators?"

Kittrell nodded. "Absolutely. Justice is what keeps us a civilized society, a free society. Without it, vengeance rules the day and we cage ourselves up in prisons of bitterness, rage, and envy."

"Who's to say we aren't already caging ourselves up with those things, Detective Kittrell?"

"At least with justice, there's an opportunity for us to live another way."

She stood up. "Unfortunately, our justice system isn't always just."

"But it tries. And that's all we can ask."

***

AN HOUR LATER, Rebecca sat in an FBI interrogation room. She took a sip of water from the glass in front of her and awaited her questioning. She'd done things wrong for a long time, but it was time to start doing things right.

The agent entered the room as he stared down at a stack of papers. He loosened his tie and sat down opposite of Rebecca. "Mrs. Westin, I'm Agent Perryman, and we appreciate you coming to us today. I know it took a lot of courage for you to come in here today, especially with all you've been through lately."

"Thanks. I needed to help a friend, and there's no use running from what I did any more."

"We're prepared to give you immunity if you tell us about your relationship with Dr. Bill Lancaster and what you did for him." He handed her a document. "You'll see all the specific details there, but the paragraph I highlighted is the important part."

She nodded and signed the document before handing it back to him.

"I'm ready to talk."

"So, tell us about your relationship with Dr. Lancaster. How did it come about?"

"About two years after I had Mason, we started trying to get pregnant, but I couldn't. So I met with a fertility specialist in Seattle right after we moved here. He recommended I reach out to Dr. Lancaster and see if he might be able to help me with some unconventional treatments."

"Did he tell you what you were taking?"

"I asked, but he told me it was best not to. Plausible deniability is what he said I needed. So for about a year, I took the supplements he sent me."

"When did you learn you were taking HGH?"

"I started to do a little research and figured out what it was."

"And you weren't worried about taking it?"

"Not at all. Even though it wasn't working, I felt great, stronger, more vibrant. I had more energy than I'd had in years. Who wouldn't keep taking something that made you feel like that?"

"But you did stop?"

"Yes, but only because I changed my mind about getting pregnant. Sid and I were having problems, and I didn't want to complicate things by having another child, especially if I was going to leave him."

"Yet you stuck with him for another three years?"

"Sid was at the end of his career then, and we didn't have a ton of money. I didn't see a bright future in that regard, and I certainly didn't see him revitalizing his career. So, I started to plan for my own future."

"And you did that by distributing HGH to local professional players?"

"Not at first. I initially thought I'd just resell my monthly allotment on the black market, but one month I accidentally got three times what I was supposed to have received. That was when I told Jonathan Umbert, Sid's agent, about it. I'd flirted with him before and told him that I was thinking about leaving Sid, but I told him it wouldn't be financially advantageous to do so. He told me he'd help get Sid a better contract. I wasn't sure that was the answer long term for me either. That's when I mentioned that I was getting extra HGH supplements that I wasn't using."

"Did he direct you toward these other players?"

"Not in the way you might think. He mentioned that he knew a few guys who might be interested and told me he could give me their contact information. When I decided to do it, he gave me all their cell phone numbers."

"How exactly did you deliver the drugs?"

"When we first moved here, Sid bought a van to help move furniture for people in impoverished areas. He'd just drive around looking for people who needed help on his days off. Nobody ever knew it was him, but it was his way of connecting with people in the community and helping out some."

"He sounds like a great guy."

"He was—just not a great husband. If you only knew—"

Agent Perryman poured himself a glass of water. "So, you used the van?"

She nodded. "I would use the van to sell ice cream in a few parks around the city. The players knew when I would be there. They bought an ice cream cone with a little something extra—the location of the dead drop with the HGH."

"Sorry I have to ask, Mrs. Westin, but did you have anything to do with your husband's death?"

She sighed. "Don't be sorry you have to ask that. I'm

sad he's gone, but I'm not sad I don't have to be married to him any more. But to answer your question—no. I had nothing to do with it. I'm convinced it was just a robbery gone awry. Sid always wanted to be the hero, whether it was on the soccer field or elsewhere."

"Did your husband know what you were doing?"

"He found out a few days before and confronted me about it. I told him I'd stop doing it."

"And were you?"

"Was I what?"

"Were you going to stop?"

She shrugged. "I hadn't decided yet, but he made a good case for me to stop. But since I didn't vow to stop on the spot, maybe that's why he decided to initiate the divorce. At that point, I honestly didn't really have any reason to continue. I'd made plenty of money, more than enough to escape him."

"Well, we're going to need that money back."

"You just gave me immunity, Agent Perryman. It's bad enough that I'm telling you everything I know about this. And now you want me to give the money back? Forget it."

"It's part of the immunity deal, Mrs. Westin. If we don't receive that money, the deal is off."

She exhaled and crossed her arms. "I thought I could trust you."

"It's no trick, Mrs. Westin. But think about it this way: It's better than going to prison and losing everything, even your son."

He handed her a piece of paper. "All we need now is the name of every athlete you sold to."

CHAPTER 37

CAL TOOK MONDAY OFF to help address the vandalism to his home. It wasn't exactly what he wanted Kelly to return home and see, but she took it in stride. She'd been on enough adventures with him to know how benign—though terrifying—the stunt was.

On his knees, Cal scrubbed the wall with a brush. Kelly stopped at the doorway to his office and was smiling when he looked up at her.

"What are you looking at?" he asked.

"This is just something I never imagined I'd see when we got married."

"What? Me cleaning a spray-painted message off the walls of my home office? If you had, I would've told you that you had a very active imagination."

She laughed. "No. Just you cleaning in general. I'm not so sure you didn't spray paint the message yourself just to avoid my wrath for the pigsty you lived in while we were gone."

"Hey, I—"

"Cal, I've seen the rest of the house. You can't blame everything on the break in." She spun and headed down the hall.

"I did bring you flowers to the airport," Cal yelled. "I need to get some credit."

His phone started buzzing, and he quickly ripped off the pair of rubber gloves he was wearing to answer the call.

"Cal, this is Jarrett Anderson."

"Agent Anderson, it's so good to hear your voice. Anything to rescue me from my current chore."

"And what might that be?"

"You wouldn't believe me if I told you."

"Try me."

"I'm on my hands and knees, cleaning a wall."

"You're right. I don't believe you."

"Would it make more sense if I told you I'm cleaning spray paint from the wall? Someone tried sending me a message yesterday."

"What kind of message?"

"The kind I get when people don't like me digging for the truth."

"Well, I'm not sure it's related, but there is a little truth I wanted to tell you about—and give you a little professional thank you."

Cal got off the floor and sat down at his desk. "What's up?"

"That article you wrote about Rebecca Westin paid off. It got all the suspects involved running scared and resulted in her giving us what we need to get a conviction of Dr. Bill Lancaster."

"How did that happen?"

"She came back to town. Felt bad about Jonathan Umbert taking the fall for those murders."

"So, he didn't do it?"

"Nope. That was all some crazy circumstantial evidence anyway. It would've never held up in court."

"Was Umbert involved?"

"He was a loose accomplice, but we'll probably scare him before we turn him loose with a warning. Besides, he'll get hit where it hurts the most anyway when some of the players he represents get suspended for illegal drug use. No need to spend the government's money to pile on him."

"Anything else?"

"Yeah, I'm emailing you the names of the athletes she supplied HGH to as we speak. Feel free to write this story but quote me only as an anonymous source. Got it?"

"Yeah. And what about Rebecca Westin? What's going to happen to her?"

"We gave her immunity, but again she wasn't the focus of our investigation. We just needed her to roll over on Dr. Lancaster. But she has to give back the money she made off the sale of the HGH."

"She won't be hurting for cash anyway. Sid had a nice insurance policy."

"As long as she wasn't behind killing him."

"You think she was?"

Anderson sighed. "I doubt it, but you never can quite tell about people, now can you?"

Cal thanked Anderson and hung up to call Buckman.

"I thought you were taking the day off," Buckman groused.

"I've got a story for you, but I want you to promise to let me write it," Cal began. "No Eddie Ramsey. Got it?"

"No promises, but what is it?"

"No promises, no story."

"Cal, you ought to know by now that you can't hold me hostage with something like that. I'm hanging up now."

"You're not going to hang up, Buckman. Your curiosity

is far greater than your pride. Tell me I can write the story, and I'll tell you what just went down."

Buckman sighed. "Fine, Cal, you win. What's the scoop?"

"Rebecca Westin just confessed to being an HGH supplier to several of the city's top star athletes."

"I thought she fled the country."

"She did, but apparently she couldn't bear the thought of Jonathan Umbert going to jail on a murder charge. She claimed to be with him at the time of the staged murder-suicide in the warehouse."

"What's going to happen to her?"

"Slap on the wrist. She gets immunity and goes free in exchange for her testimony of Dr. Bill Lancaster, who was the target of the FBI's investigation all along."

"Well, that's all well and good, but the bigger story still remains: Who murdered those men, and was Sid Westin's murder premeditated or just wrong place, wrong time?"

"I'm assuming you still want this story though, right?"

"You've got one hour to file it—then I want you to get back on the Sid Westin story."

Cal smiled. "Why the change of heart?"

"Your story on yesterday's boat race was a steaming pile of shit—and Ramsey couldn't find a source if it hit him over the head."

"You won't regret this."

"I think I already am."

***

CAL POUNDED OUT HIS STORY and needed to get confirmation from Detective Kittrell about a few details, particularly if Jonathan Umbert had been released.

"Yes, we released him about a half hour ago," Kittrell told Cal over the phone. "I swear I don't know how you find out about this stuff so quickly."

"So nobody else knows?"

"We haven't put out a press release yet, if that's what you mean. Chief Roman isn't too fond of trumpeting faulty arrests."

"What about the murder-suicide with the bank robbers? Anything there yet?"

"Not yet. I'm moving slow these days with Quinn still out sick. But the department's position is that it was staged and the killer is still out there. We don't think he's a danger to anyone. Heck, I don't mind if he takes out a few more of these low-life scumbags. But that's all we know at this point."

"Thanks for all this. I have a feeling we're not done working together."

"Not by a long shot—at least, not until we catch this killer. Until then, we won't have any answers about Sid Westin."

Cal hung up and finished writing his story. He filed it with *The Times* and returned to scrubbing the walls.

He'd only been back at it a few minutes when Kelly stopped in the doorway again. "Still scrubbing the same wall? Good thing you write for a living. We'd all starve if you were a professional wall scrubber."

"For the record, I had some business to attend to."

She smiled and shook her head. "You've always got some excuse."

"I'm not kidding."

Cal's phone buzzed again.

She pointed at his phone. "Looks like you've got some

more business to attend." She paused as he took off his gloves. "Just wondering if you asked your friends to call you so you could get out of this."

Cal waved her off dismissively. "Ever the comedian."

She disappeared down the hall, and Cal answered the phone.

"This is Cal Murphy."

"Cal, this is Javier Martinez."

"Good to hear from you, Javy. What's going on?"

"Well, I found something I thought you might be interested in."

"What is it?"

"There's something I need to show you. I'll text you the location and meet you there in an hour."

CHAPTER 38

CAL PULLED INTO THE PARKING LOT of a vacated Wal-Mart just a few miles from the Seattle FC practice facility. Developers had bet heavily on this bedroom community of Seattle becoming the next big housing boon, but local city council quarrels left infrastructure projects dangling, and it never really got off the ground. A stiff breeze whipped around the plastic covering of a half-finished fast-food restaurant located at the corner of the lot near the road. Like the massive box store that closed its doors three months ago, it too now sat abandoned.

Cal got out of his car and looked for Martinez, but he wasn't there. He leaned against his car and tried to soak up some of the intermittent sunshine. After a few minutes, he decided to retreat back into his car. He checked his phone again and noted the time. Martinez was fifteen minutes late, and Cal was beginning to wonder if he was coming at all.

Just as Cal had decided to call him back, Martinez roared up next to him in the lot in his red Ferrari FF. They both got out of their cars.

"Sorry I'm late," Martinez said. "I had to take my mom to the store to buy her groceries this week."

"Javy, the good son," Cal said with a laugh. Then he

stopped and admired Martinez's car. "I always wondered whose car this was."

Martinez smiled. "She's my pride and joy."

"But a four-seater?"

"The more the merrier, I say." He paused. "Plus, sometimes I have to drive both my parents around at the same time."

"A practical man," Cal said. "That's why I like you, Javy. You always have a good reason for everything you do."

"I'm glad you feel that way, and I hope you understand why I've got a good reason for giving you this."

Martinez reached into his pocket, fished out a cell phone, and handed it to Cal.

"What's this?" Cal said as he took the phone.

"It's Sid Westin's phone."

Cal furrowed his brow. "The police report said he had his phone on him."

"I'm sure he did, but he didn't have that phone on him. It was his special burner phone. We went out to lunch after practice the day he was killed, and he must've left it in my car."

"Why would he have a burner phone?" Cal said as he inspected the device.

"Sometimes you think you know someone, but then you have no idea."

"Javy, what are you not telling me?"

"I don't know anything you don't already know about him. Think, Cal. This was his phone for his honeys."

"Was he really that much of a philanderer?"

"Legendary."

"Then how come there wasn't more about it in the tabloids or on the Internet?"

Martinez shrugged. "Some people are better at covering their tracks than others. But he still got caught from time to time."

Cal held up the phone. "So, what's on here?"

"Why don't you see for yourself?"

Cal turned on the phone and started scrolling through the media files. No contacts. No photos. Just one lone video. "Did you watch this?"

"There's nothing to see, but you should listen to it."

Cal started the video, which remained black throughout. He figured Sid must've covertly turned on the recording in his pocket.

First came Sid's voice. He sounded angry and upset. But not as angry as the voice of the other person, who began to berate him.

"Is that whose voice I think it is?" Cal asked, his mouth agape.

Martinez nodded. "There's only one guy on our team who talks like that. It's undeniable."

CHAPTER 39

KITTRELL SHUFFLED INTO HIS OFFICE on Tuesday morning and braced for an earful from Chief Roman. It's not like Kittrell didn't deserve it. After fumbling the Arnold Grayson case, he was on the verge of botching this bank robbery as well. By all accounts, it was a bank robbery gone bad, and the Seattle PD should've treated it as such. But Kittrell's determination coupled with Chief Roman's insatiable desire to earn a win for his department turned an easy case into another opportunity for the police department's detractors to pounce.

And Roman hated public derision.

Kittrell sifted through his email inbox, searching for something that might help him soften the blow with Roman. Nothing.

The phone on his desk then beeped. He glanced at the caller ID but didn't need to. It was Roman.

"Get into my office right now," Roman growled. "We need to have a little talk."

During his trek to Roman's office, he tried to think of a plausible excuse. The most obvious one was that he'd been working without his partner, Quinn, who was still sick—though Kittrell began to wonder if he wasn't actually in

Puerto Vallarta on vacation. For a second, it sounded good. But after he thought about it longer, it was lame. It was just an excuse. And the only thing Roman hated more than public derision was excuses.

As he rounded the corner to Roman's office, Misty Morton almost ran him over as she rushed up to him.

"Detective Kittrell, I'm so glad I caught you," she said as she gasped for air.

He stopped, keeping one eye on Roman, who seemed engaged in paperwork. "Why? What is it?"

"I did some more digging on Robert Fisher, and guess what I found?"

"Don't keep me in suspense."

"I found out he has another alias—Ty Pullman."

"Am I supposed to know who he is?"

"The department has been trying to nail him for years. He's allegedly one of William Lynch's top goons."

"But robbing banks isn't Lynch's standard MO. He's usually extorting people and making them give him money."

She wrinkled her face. "Well, that's what we think is Lynch's MO. Maybe he's more violent than we give him credit for."

"That would be a shift."

"Perhaps. But maybe not because there's more. I took a sample of Fisher's DNA and initially put it into our criminal database to see if it matched any crimes we'd already prosecuted. Nothing. Then this morning, I decided to cross-check it against unsolved cases."

"And?"

"I found a match," she said as she handed Kittrell a printout.

"Can this be right?"

"Can and is right," she said as a grin spread across her face. "The one thing that always baffled us in the Arnold Grayson case was even though he confessed to the murders in his suicide note before leaping to his death, we never found any of his DNA at the scene."

"Perhaps he was extra careful."

"That's a possibility. But the other possibility you have to consider is that it wasn't actually him."

"And you think that's the case here?"

She nodded. "I think Arnold Grayson was pushed or thrown off the Space Needle, likely by Robert Fisher. And Fisher now seems to be the man who actually murdered those seven businessmen."

"That's quite a leap—no pun intended."

"So you think William Lynch was behind all this?"

"That's what the evidence points to. I mean, I don't think Fisher was out on some personal killing vendetta."

"In other words, the robbery was indeed a cover to murder Westin."

She nodded. "Uh-huh."

"The problem is I can't question the suspect, who killed our victim."

"Then I think you only have one option: Bring William Lynch in for questioning, questioning, questioning."

"Cute," Kittrell quipped. "You're not the one who has to break all this news to Chief."

"That's why you get paid the big bucks, Detective." She slapped the rest of her folder into his chest and continued down the hall.

"Kittrell, get in here now!" bellowed Roman.

Kittrell stared at the folder in his hand as he tried to figure out a way to tell Roman the good news that his boss would inevitably take as bad news. Detaining and questioning someone of William Lynch's stature wasn't something the chief would consider lightly—and it wasn't something the department could keep quiet.

Kittrell settled into the chair opposite of Roman and finally looked up.

"What's the matter, Kittrell? You look like someone just shot your dog."

"This is not the face of someone whose dog just got shot, but it is the face of someone who wants to reopen a case."

"Why don't you finish the one you've got first?"

"I think they might be connected."

Roman's eyes narrowed. "What case are you talking about?"

"The Arnold Grayson case."

Roman threw his hands in the air and let out a string of expletives. "Do you pick at your scabs, Kittrell? Because I had two kids who couldn't leave well enough alone when it came to their boo-boos. They would pick and pick and pick, sometimes for months on end. And eventually—boom! They'd start bleeding again, moaning and wailing like they'd been shot. Their mother would go cuckoo, running around the house, arms flailing. Sometimes I wasn't sure if they were the ones who got hurt or if she was. And I'm this close to turning into channeling my wife and going crazy. Now just stop it with these shenanigans. That case is closed. You blew it. Now get over it and solve this next one."

Kittrell pushed the folder across the desk toward Roman. "Chief, do you realize we never found Grayson's DNA at any of the crime scenes? Now how is that even possible? Those were violent murders."

"Murders with guns and knives that all carried Grayson's fingerprints on them."

"Don't you think that due to the violent nature of those murders, we would've found his DNA at least once at those crime scenes?"

"That's a fair question, but it's not one that's begging to be asked by anyone. Besides, even if you're able to prove it was Fisher and not Grayson, what good does that do anyone? You're just dredging up wounds for all those victims' families—and Grayson's family as well."

"I bet Grayson's family would appreciate knowing their loved one was murdered, too, instead of being forever labeled a murderer."

"Fair enough. But I don't see how that is all connected to this armed robbery and potentially Sid Westin's death."

"William Lynch."

"What does he have to do with all this?"

"Fisher is one of Lynch's right hand men."

Roman threw his hands in the air. "Are you trying to get us all fired, Kittrell? Parading him in here is the last thing we need."

"Only if you don't want to find out the truth."

Roman sighed and stared past Kittrell for a moment. "Okay, fine. You can question him—but not here. You go on site and question him in his office, but be discreet. Then if you think we should bring him, we'll talk about it."

Kittrell nodded and stood up, turning toward the door.

"Good work, Detective," Roman said with a faint smile. "I look forward to seeing what you come back with."

Kittrell sat down at his desk, where a package rested on top of his keyboard. He called the front desk. "Felicia, what is this package doing on my desk?"

"Cal Murphy dropped it by. He told me to give it to you. It's a burner phone that supposedly belonged to Sid Westin." She paused. "He didn't tell you about this?"

"No, but thanks. I'll contact him."

Less than a minute later, he was smiling as he strode into Molly Morton's office. "Got a present for you."

She spun around in her chair. "It's going to take more than a smile to get me to look at that for you—especially sometime this century."

"Grande soy latte?" he said as he pointed at her.

"Now you're talking my language." She winked at him. "I'll see what I can do."

CHAPTER 40

MATT NORFOLK FLIPPED THE BALL into the air and juggled it on his foot a few times before whirling and kicking it from midfield into the upper right corner of the goal. The rest of his Seattle FC teammates had retreated to the locker room fifteen minutes ago when practice ended. But Norfolk wasn't ready to quit. He'd sacrificed so much already just to reach this point in his career—and he wasn't about to fall behind again.

He started to repeat the drill when he heard a commotion coming from behind him at the other end of the field. Straining to make out who it was, he identified the Seattle FC media relations director, Paul Holloway, sparring verbally with another man. Holloway failed in his efforts to stop the man who evaded him. As the man walked in Norfolk's direction, he recognized him: Cal Murphy.

"I'm not going to ask you to stop again," Holloway yelled at Cal.

"Good!" Cal said as he continued to march toward the middle of the field.

"I mean it. I'm going to call security and have them escort you off the premises. You're not welcome here."

"Excellent. That will make for some great social media

viewing since I'm recording everything right now."

"I told Buckman your credentials have been revoked," Holloway said.

Half annoyed, half intrigued, Norfolk jogged in Cal's direction. He waved at Holloway. "It's okay, Paul. I'll talk to him. I'm sure you have better things to do. He's harmless."

Norfolk watched Holloway huff and storm off. He then turned his attention toward Cal. "What brings you out here today, Mr. Murphy? Not enough muck to rake with the Mariners in Spring Training this week?"

Cal threw his hands up. "What can I say? I'm impartial to the beautiful game."

"No, you're impartial to the mystery behind Sid Westin's death even though there's no mystery any more. Wrong place, wrong time. It was unfortunate."

"Yet you benefit more than anybody with his death."

Norfolk began to juggle the ball on his foot. "It was only a matter of time before I overtook the old man anyway. He struggled in training and hadn't lasted an entire game this season. He was on his last leg. If he didn't get out of the way for me, he was going to get run over."

"I appreciate your confidence—I really do. But you and I both know your coach wasn't going to replace Sid with you. He was a legend."

"Maybe you're right. But they wouldn't let me get away either. I'm the future of this club. They need me."

"He was a legend—and you are in your own mind."

"Did you just come all the way out here to insult me? I can call Paul back out here to have security escort you back to your car."

Cal held up both hands in a posture of surrender. "I come in peace."

"Then why don't you act like it and get to the point of your visit." Norfolk popped the ball in the air and kicked it into the goal.

"The reason I'm here is I actually don't believe the person responsible for Sid's death has been found."

"What about the guy who shot him? Isn't he dead?"

"True. But he was just a pawn. Somebody hired him, and I think I might know whom. But I wanted to ask you a few questions."

Before Cal could say another word, Shawn Lynch, with his nasally voice, yelled at Norfolk. "You want to go to lunch today?"

Norfolk waved him off. "I'm good. I'll catch you tomorrow." He returned his gaze toward Cal, who stared at Lynch, mouth agape. "You were saying—"

Cal refocused his attention on Norfolk. "Oh, sorry. I was saying that I wanted to ask you a few questions."

Norfolk started to juggle another ball on his foot. "I know, I know. Get to them, okay? I still want to get some more drills in here."

"Do you ever feel like there are some guys on this team who don't pull their weight?"

"What do you mean?"

"I mean, are there some guys who seem to vanish mentally in the middle of a game?"

"We all do that sometimes. But are there some guys who do it more often than others?" Norfolk nodded. "Yeah. There are a few of those."

"What about him?" Cal said, pointing at Lynch, who was climbing into his car. "Does he do that sometimes?"

"He's one of the biggest offenders," Norfolk said, nodding in Lynch's direction. "But that's not unusual for one of the new guys on the team. It's an adjustment."

"But you don't have that problem?"

"The fact that I'm aware that an issue often exists ought to tell you all you need to know about my preparedness as a player."

"Duly noted," Cal said as he scratched down some notes on his pad. "Now, I promise not to quote you directly on this, but do you think Lynch would benefit from Sid being dead? Like, for example, would he get more endorsements? Because he's already starting."

Norfolk shrugged. "Maybe. Sid was certainly hogging all the endorsements."

"Last question. Do you think he was capable of pulling off something like what happened to Sid?"

Norfolk looked at him incredulously. "You mean hiring a hit man to kill him during a bank robbery? Is that what you're asking me?"

Cal nodded.

"I guess so, but he's far from the coldest player on this team and the one I would suspect if I were investigating Sid's death as a murder."

"Well, out with it then."

CHAPTER 41

THE CORPORATE HEADQUARTERS of Cars, Cars, Cars was far less assuming than Kittrell imagined. The way it was presented on television, Kittrell believed the company's office space had to look like a scaled-down version of the Taj Mahal, complete with gold fenders and platinum bumpers adorned on the walls. Instead, it was rather modest with little more than art prints hung from the walls and un-comfortable—and mismatched—furniture used to decorate the waiting area.

Kittrell glanced at his phone and waited to be summoned by the sassy receptionist, who looked over the top of her glasses at everyone.

"Detective Mel Kittrell," she called. "Mr. Lynch will see you now."

She pointed to her right where a young man was waiting for him. He greeted Kittrell with a smile. "Thank you for stopping by, sir. Right this way."

Kittrell followed the man through a set of double doors and into an expansive office where William Lynch sat pecking away on his computer keyboard.

"Have a seat," Lynch muttered as he continued to pound away.

Kittrell sat down. "Thank you, Mr. Lynch."

After a few moments, Lynch looked up. "So, what is it you're here to see me about, Detective?"

Kittrell almost burst into laughter at the absurd portrait someone had painted of Lynch and his Pomeranian centered on the wall behind him. It wasn't the portrait itself as much as it was the look on Lynch's face—and how it matched the dog's. They both peered down their noses, and it was exactly how Kittrell felt in that moment, as if Lynch was giving him the once over without considering what he had to say.

"How well did you know Robert Fisher?"

Lynch knit his brow. "Who?"

"Robert Fisher."

"Never heard of him," Lynch scoffed.

"Are you sure about that?" Kittrell countered. "Apparently, he worked for you for quite a number of years."

"Oh, yes, Bobby Fisher. We used to call him that and tease him because he shared the same name as the great chess player. But let me tell you, our Bobby Fisher couldn't get his opponent into check if his life depended on it, let alone understand the concept of checkmate."

"And what exactly did he do for you?"

Lynch leaned back in his chair. "Why all the interest in Fisher? What did he do?"

"He's dead," Kittrell said, devoid of any feeling or emotion.

"Dead?"

"I didn't stutter. He's dead, sir."

Lynch put his hands behind his head, interlocking his fingers. He stared at the ceiling and appeared to choke back a few tears. It was all believable theater that Kittrell appreciated, even if he didn't believe Lynch was being truthful.

"Good ole Bobby Fisher is dead."

"As a doornail." Kittrell paused. "Don't you read the paper?"

"Only to figure out how to place my bets."

"Fair enough. So, what I came here to ask you is why did your organization donate more than two hundred grand into an offshore account with Robert Fisher's name on it?"

Lynch sighed. "I don't know, Detective. Does it look like I've got time to micromanage my people around here? I'm too busy building an empire to worry about who got what and how much. Maybe he did; maybe he didn't. You'll have to ask someone in accounting about that."

"So, for the record, you're saying you had nothing to do with it?"

"For the record, I barely know who Robert Fisher is."

Kittrell was persistent. "So, you're denying any involvement with Fisher in his attempt to rob Puget Sound Bank a little over a week ago?"

"I'm saying I hardly know who Fisher is, and I'd never ask him to do such a thing. If he was involved, it wasn't on my behalf."

Kittrell stood up. "Sorry to take up so much of your time, sir. If you ever need any help at the department, please let me know."

Lynch chuckled. "Oh, yes. I've got a few suggestions for you, starting with Cal Murphy. If there's any way you can get him tarred and feathered for suggesting that my son used HGH to make it to the high level of professional soccer in the U.S., that'd be great."

"I'm a detective, sir, not a miracle worker."

"Whatever you do, keep me posted. Understood?"

Kittrell nodded. "I'll update you when I have a chance."

He stood up. "And thank you for your time, sir."

Lynch nodded back. "And, Detective? If you still think someone else was behind it all, I know exactly where you need to turn your focus."

CHAPTER 42

CAL MET KITTRELL DOWNTOWN at the main precinct, both men eager to share with one another what they found and discuss the case. With Quinn gone, Cal felt like he was serving more as a substitute partner than a consultant.

"Is Chief Roman still okay with me consulting on this case?" Cal asked.

"At this point, what difference does it make? I think he'd approve of a cat being my partner if it meant we could close out this case."

"Not a dog?"

"Some guys already have dogs as partners, had to be creative with my analogy."

Cal chuckled. "Maybe you should be the writer then."

"I hate writing reports. I couldn't imagine how much I'd hate trying to write a book."

"To each his own," Cal said, pulling out his notepad. "So, did you get a chance to listen to the recording on that phone I dropped off?"

"I'm about three hours ahead of you here and have a truckload of information to share with you. But first things first: I had Molly play the recording for me on my way back from visiting William Lynch."

"And?"

"And it sounded like Shawn Lynch to me, but I had her do a little digging on the phone."

"Like looking for numbers and prints?"

"A little more advanced than that, starting with the recording itself."

Cal leaned forward in his chair. "What do you mean?"

"I mean, something sounded off about it, like it was faked."

"And what did she find out?"

Kittrell cracked his knuckles and looked Cal in the eyes. "That conversation never happened. It was all digitally reconstructed."

"Was there anything else on the phone of use?"

"At first Molly said it looked clean, but she took a second pass at it and found another file. People often make the mistake of thinking that when they delete something on their phone, it's completely gone from the memory, but that's not always the case. It's gone forever when it gets recorded on top of. But when a phone has hardly any information stored on it, files are stored in fresh locations."

"Meaning there was another conversation?"

Kittrell nodded and pulled out a thumb drive and then plugged it into his computer. "Listen to this." He hit play and let the recording roll. It was Sid Westin talking with Javier Martinez.

> **Sid:** Javy, I've got a friend who's been doing a little analytics for me.
> **Martinez:** Is it helping your game at all?
> **Sid:** A little bit. It's made me think about my tendencies and be more pro-active about going left

more often than always going right when I have the ball in the area. But that's not the most interesting thing he's discovered.

Martinez: What was then?

Sid: He showed me a spreadsheet detailing games we were favored in and the final outcome.

Martinez: And that was more interesting?

Sid: Only because it was also overlaid with each player's performance metrics. And you know what he found?

(No response from Martinez)

Sid: He found that in certain games where we were favored by two goals or more, you under-performed and we only won those games by one goal, sometimes tying. And then in certain games when we were predicted to lose by two goals or more, your performance exceeded your usual metrics. Oftentimes, we won those games or tied. Then he called a friend of his who runs one of Lynch's underground gambling rings, and you know what he found?

(Still no response from Martinez)

Sid: He found that those games where you per-formed differently than normal, there was an above average amount of money bet on those games—which got me to thinking. I know you used to work for William Lynch and your father still does. If this is some way to get back at him, I'm going to tell you right now that it's a danger-ous game you're playing.

Martinez: You don't know what you're talking about.

Sid: The numbers don't lie, Javy. This isn't something to play around with. Lynch is a dangerous man. You think Shawn really made this team on his own merit?

Martinez: Maybe Shawn did, and maybe he didn't. But whatever you think I'm doing, you're wrong.

Sid: If it happens again, I'm going to the authorities—or William Lynch himself. I'm sure he'd love to know he's being hustled.

Martinez: I know what it might look like, but it's not what you think. It's complicated.

Sid: It's always complicated—so uncomplicate it. Do the right thing. People on this team are counting on you. We want to win a championship, and we'll never be able to with a teammate who's jerking us around like this.

Martinez: Just worry about yourself.

Kittrell turned the recording off and looked at Cal.

"Why would Javy give me the phone with that information on there? It doesn't make sense," Cal said.

"It makes perfect sense if he thinks he's going to send you off in the wrong direction. This investigation has a shelf life, and if it's not solved, we're going to move on."

"But why would he use the same phone?"

"Maybe he thought we'd be able to trace it back to its owner and he didn't want to get caught in a cover up."

"Too late for that now."

Kittrell nodded. "The problem we have now is admissibility. Would a judge allow this to be heard in court? If not, the prosecution would be sunk and he'd walk."

"You really think he'd kill Sid over this? They were best friends on the team."

"Which is why he had to hire someone to kill him—one of his best friends growing up. Now, Robert Fisher used to be known as Ty Pullman, Javier Martinez's next-door neighbor. The two boys apparently spent a lot of time together down at the docks as well as away from them, getting into mischief mostly. They were both arrested for some minor things like breaking and entering and vandalism, but nothing violent."

"But I know Martinez respected Sid. What would drive him to have him murdered?"

Kittrell held his finger up. "That's the one area we're still trying to figure out. But once we do, this case will be a slam dunk."

"As long as you can use that conversation with Sid."

"Exactly. But that's easier said than done."

Cal stood up and exhaled a long breath. "I think I've got an idea how we can solve both those problems in one fell swoop."

CHAPTER 43

CAL SAT IN THE SMALL SET of aluminum bleachers at midfield of the Seattle FC practice complex. He checked his watch. Javier Martinez was two minutes late, and he was never late for an appointment. Cal began to get nervous, fiddling with his shirt.

He looked at his watch again. Now Martinez was three minutes late.

Cal started to wonder if his brilliant idea was a bust.

Two minutes later, Martinez roared into the parking lot in his Ferrari FF. He coolly grabbed his bag out of the back and started the trek from the parking lot to the bleachers where Cal sat alone.

A strong breeze held the U.S. flag and the team flag almost stiff in the wind. Cal glanced at his watch again.

What's taking him so long to walk over here?

Once Martinez arrived, he slid onto the bench next to Cal. "Where's Shawn?" Martinez asked.

Cal looked at his watch again. "He should be here any minute." He glanced at Martinez's bag. "You going to get in some extra reps after this?"

"I might as well since I'm out here. You can never be too prepared."

Cal cleared his throat and shifted his weight from side to side on the bench. He could feel his palms beginning to exude sweat. He took a deep breath. "Before Shawn gets here, I want us to listen to that recording you gave me."

"Is that necessary?" Martinez asked.

"It is if we want to be prepared. The best way to catch him is in his own words."

Martinez nodded reluctantly. "Go ahead then."

Cal held out the burner phone Martinez had given him and called up the actual recording Molly Morton had discovered. Then he pressed play.

Eyeing Martinez carefully, Cal watched Martinez's eyes widen once he realized it was his voice with Sid's instead of the one he put onto the phone.

"Where did you get this?" Martinez said as he picked it up after the recording ended. "This has to be faked. That's not my voice."

"I'm afraid it is, but you already knew that, Javy."

"Look, I don't know what kind of stunt you're trying to pull here, but this isn't cool. I've done nothing but help you try to solve this case—if there even is one—and now you've concocted some story that places the blame on me."

Cal began to clap slowly. "I always knew soccer players were good actors, rolling around on the ground like someone shot their knee cap when there isn't even any contact. But you? You, Javier Martinez, should be nominated for an Oscar with that performance right there. It's so believable."

"That's because it is believable, Cal."

"Don't try to play me for the fool. I've been around long enough to know a rat when I see one. Heck, I don't even have to see them; I can just smell them. And you're a rat."

"You've gotta believe me, Cal. Sid was my best friend.

Someone planted that evidence on me."

Cal cocked his head to one side and pointed at Martinez. "I'd almost believe you if I didn't know better, like, say, that Robert Fisher's real name is Ty Pullman and he lived next door to you growing up. And if I didn't know that both your fathers worked for William Lynch—and both undoubtedly hated him, though Fisher went and landed a job with Lynch doing his dirty work."

"You're crazy."

Cal shrugged. "Perhaps, but I think the better possibility here is the fact that you pulled off a brilliant plot and almost got away with it." He stood up and started to pace in front of the bleachers, steepling his hands as he looked down and continued speaking. "You even had some guys rough me up on Saturday morning, but not before you sent a couple of old guys in to sit next to me and pretend to get my attention and fill my head with stories about the evil Mr. Lynch and what he used to do to people on the docks—which I actually believe were true. But then you had to push your luck in an effort to cast aspersions on Shawn Lynch by faking a recording that made it seem like Sid found out about Shawn using a PED. With everything we'd already published in the paper about the FBI's case with Rebecca Westin and HGH, you assumed that it'd be easy to lump Shawn Lynch into that story and make it all believable. And it almost was, except for a few key elements."

Cal stopped and held up his index finger. "First, you didn't know that Rebecca Westin already gave the authorities a full list of every athlete she sold drugs to—and Shawn Lynch's name wasn't on the list. Secondly, and your most critical mistake, was that you gave us Sid's original burner phone, which had the original conversation that gave you—

and you alone—motive. You killed three men at that warehouse, including your friend Ty. And you even managed to pay someone to kill the other robber in prison. But what angers me the most is that you came into my house and tried to threaten me."

Martinez unzipped his bag and fished around in it for a second, pulling out an object that he hid behind his back from Cal. "Perhaps you should've been a detective instead of a journalist. Too bad no one will ever read this story."

Realizing what was happening, Cal spun and started sprinting toward his car. He heard Martinez's footsteps getting closer and closer with each passing second. Glancing over his shoulder to see what Martinez had in his hand, he was somewhat relieved to know it was a knife instead of a gun, but that didn't change the fact that Cal was in grave danger.

Cal pumped his fists and could almost hear Martinez breathing down his neck. Then a swipe, nicking Cal's right arm and sending blood everywhere. Then another swipe at his left arm. And then a thud.

Cal didn't stop running, but he looked behind him to see what happened. Martinez had tumbled to the ground, and a ball bounced a few meters away. Then another ball came flying in Martinez's direction. Cal had turned his attention straight ahead but heard the ball hit hard off Martinez's back.

As Cal neared the fence exiting the practice field, he spied a slew of agents racing toward him.

"Took you long enough," Cal said to one of the men, who grabbed him and pulled him over to the side. "He could've killed me."

"But he didn't," the officer said, devoid of emotion.

Cal watched as the squad sprinted onto the field toward

Martinez and hemmed him in. Less than thirty seconds later, Martinez was lying face down on the turf with one officer securing his hands behind his back with handcuffs. Cal remained in his position until they brought Martinez by.

Cal held up his hand, motioning for the officers to stop. They turned Martinez so he was facing Cal.

"Why'd you do it, Javy? I know you and Sid were friends. How could you?"

"Her blood is on your hands now," Martinez hissed. "It's on your hands."

"Whose blood?"

"My mother's. Now's she's going die because of you. William Lynch owned that house we lived in, and it was built using materials nobody should have to live around. Asbestos, lead in the pipes and paint; it was a death trap. And it all caught up with my mother."

"Javy, there are lawyers who could've helped you."

"They did help. She won a settlement out of court to pay her medical fees. But when the cancer returned, she couldn't sue them again. A doctor on Lynch's payroll declared her cancer free, which meant any return would be on her dime now. The only way I could make enough money to help get her the treatment she needs to survive is expensive—and I can't even afford it. Her insurance won't pay for it, so she's left to fend for herself. And I wasn't about to let my mother die like that." He choked back a few tears. "Cal, have you ever seen someone die of cancer?"

Cal nodded.

"So you know. It's brutal. And now my mother will endure all that pain—and all because of that greedy bastard William Lynch."

Cal looked sympathetically at Martinez. "I'll take care of

your mother; don't you worry about that." Cal sighed. "But you had someone murdered. And that I can't help you with."

He nodded at the guards, who resumed marching Martinez toward several squad cars.

"Great work, Detective," came a voice behind Cal. He turned around to see Quinn standing next to Kittrell. "Don't think this is going to be a permanent thing for you."

Cal laughed and pointed at Quinn. "I hope you're feeling better because this is a job I don't want." Cal turned and looked at Kittrell. "And how long were you going to wait before you came to give me a hand? I could've gotten killed out there."

Kittrell reached up Cal's shirt and snatched the wire off his chest.

"Ouch! A little warning would've been nice," Cal said.

Kittrell snickered. "But, Cal, it's the element of surprise that made your little operation work."

"Little? I was able to save evidence that would've otherwise been thrown out for the prosecution and unearthed Martinez's motive. I'd say that was huge."

"Either way, good work. I'm glad you agreed to consult with us. You'd make a great detective."

Cal smiled. "Thanks—and you just might make a good writer, too."

CHAPTER 44

CAL NEVER IMAGINED his determination to prove that Sid Westin's death would unravel the city like it did. In his article detailing the plot, he also revealed another scoop Kittrell gave him: The seven businessmen who were supposedly killed by Arnold Grayson were believed to have been killed by Robert Fisher, the alias for Ty Pullman. He made sure to give Kittrell full credit for solving the crime and coerced the editor to pen an apology on the opinion page for chastising Kittrell and Quinn in the past as the "Keystone Cops." But that wasn't all.

The story that sent shockwaves throughout the city was the revelation of William Lynch's underground gambling ring. Whatever friends Lynch had in Seattle law enforcement who were protecting him from getting exposed couldn't any longer. Lynch couldn't escape the weight of justice and landed in prison with a twenty-year sentence.

Meanwhile, Dr. Bill Lancaster wound up getting his day in court with the feds and lost. He was sentenced to a ten-year term.

The flurry of periphery stories that cropped up around the case kept Cal busy for a week, including the revelation that Tim Peterson did indeed flunk a drug test. When the last one was finally written, he was about to invite Buckman and Ramsey to join him for a beer at King's Hardware when Alicia Westin called.

"Mr. Murphy?" she said after he answered.

"Please, call me Cal."

"Okay, Cal. I wanted to thank you for everything you did in uncovering my brother's killer. It wasn't who we thought it was, but we thought someone was behind it all."

"And you were right."

"I know this simple phone call isn't enough to truly thank you for what you did, but my entire family is grateful."

"I'm just doing my job."

"Well, thank you—and I mean that from the bottom of my heart."

Cal hung up and took a deep breath. It was those moments that made what he did worth it.

He scanned the newsroom again and spotted the targets of his impending invite to King's Hardware.

A half-hour later, Cal bought Buckman and Ramsey a round of beers and swallowed hard before starting to speak, "I brought you two here today to say thank you and sorry. Thank you for believing in me, Buckman. I know this story was a crazy one, and I had to sound like a fool as I insisted it appeared to be murder, but you still believed in me." Cal turned to Ramsey. "And, Ramsey, I was the biggest jackass this side of the Mississippi, and I want to tell you that I'm sorry. I should've never treated you that way, and you did an admirable job under the circumstances of picking up my pieces and writing a couple of solid stories. Even though I was upset about the story you broke on Umbert being a suspect in the murder-for-hire plot to kill Westin—and even though you were wrong," Cal said with a wink, "it was good reporting. And I promise that I'll do my best in the future not to treat you like that again."

Ramsey held up his mug and clinked it with Cal's and then Buckman's. "All is forgiven."

In the middle of throwing down the rest of his beer, Cal froze when the bar fell silent. He slowly put his glass down and realized everyone was staring at the television.

In a developing story, we've just learned that Mike Black, the starting strong safety for the Seahawks is in critical condition after being shot earlier this evening.

Cal slapped a ten-dollar bill on the table and put on his coat. "Well, guys, it looks like it's back to work."

###

ACKNOWLEDGMENTS

AS A FIVE-YEAR-OLD BOY living in England I never had a chance not to play soccer, the world's beautiful game. And I became hooked. Even after my family moved back to the United States, I withstood plenty of ridicule and scorn for my love for soccer. Watching soccer develop in the U.S. has been fascinating — and it truly has reached a fever pitch level in the cities where there are professional teams.

I'd like to thank Margo Yoder, who helped shape this story into something better through her keen eye for detail, as well as Krystal Wade, whose editing skills helped take this wrinkled shirt of a story and press it smooth. And Dan Pitts did another wonderful job in capturing the look and feel of Cuba for the cover.

Bill Cooper continues to crank out stellar audio versions of all my books — and I have no doubt that this will yield the same high-quality listening enjoyment.

And to you the reader—thanks for reading!

ABOUT THE AUTHOR

R.J. PATTERSON is an award-winning writer living in southeastern Idaho. He first began his illustrious writing career as a sports journalist, recording his exploits on the soccer fields in England as a young boy. Then when his father told him that people would pay him to watch sports if he would write about what he saw, he went all in. He landed his first writing job at age 15 as a sports writer for a daily newspaper in Orangeburg, S.C. He later earned a degree in newspaper journalism from the University of Georgia, where he took a job covering high school sports for the award-winning *Athens Banner-Herald* and *Daily News*.

He later became the sports editor at a daily newspaper in south Georgia before working in the magazine world as an editor and freelance journalist. He has won numerous writing awards, including a national award for his investigative reporting on a sordid tale surrounding an NCAA investigation over the University of Georgia football program.

R.J. enjoys the great outdoors of the Northwest while living there with his wife and three children. He still follows sports closely.

He also loves connecting with readers and would love to hear from you. To stay updated about future projects, connect with him over Facebook or on the Internet at www.IamJackPatterson.com

Made in the USA
San Bernardino, CA
17 November 2019